A Stolen Shadow

A STOLEN SHADOW

A CHIEF INSPECTOR SHADOW MYSTERY

H L Marsay

A Stolen Shadow
Copyright© 2024 H L Marsay
Tule Publishing First Printing, January 2024

The Tule Publishing, Inc.

ALL RIGHTS RESERVED

First Publication by Tule Publishing 2024

Cover design by Patrick Knowles

No part of this book may be used or reproduced in any manner whatsoever without written permission except in the case of brief quotations embodied in critical articles and reviews.

This is a work of fiction. Names, characters, places, and incidents are products of the author's imagination or are used fictitiously. Any resemblance to actual events, locales, organizations, or persons, living or dead, is entirely coincidental.

AI was not used to create any part of this book and no part of this book may be used for generative training.

ISBN: 978-1-961544-72-7

Dedication

We lost our two beautiful dogs within three months of each other, between December 2022 and March 2023. This is the first book I have written without my ever-present companions sighing and snoring at my feet or loudly interrupting me whenever a squirrel trespassed into the garden.

I would like to dedicate *A Stolen Shadow* to all the other dogs out there who are keeping their authors company. You make the lonely business of writing much more fun.

Author's Note

A Stolen Shadow includes Shadow and Jimmy watching a performance of the pantomime *Snow White*. For any non-UK-based readers who are not familiar with pantomimes, I thought a brief explanation might be helpful.

Pantomimes are a form of family entertainment and are traditionally staged after Christmas. They are usually based around a fairy tale or folk story such as *Cinderella*, *Jack and the Beanstalk* or *Robin Hood* and feature familiar characters including a pantomime dame (a middle-aged man in drag) and a pantomime horse or cow (two actors in an animal costume). There are musical numbers, dancing, slapstick comedy, lots of jokes and double entendres.

Audience participation is a big part of pantomime. Sweets are often thrown from the stage, and those watching are encouraged to join in with singing, to boo and hiss whenever the villain appears and call out phrases like, "He's behind you!" or whenever a character says "Oh yes it is," the audience responds with "Oh no it isn't."

As readers of other books in this series can probably guess, Shadow is not a fan of the pantomime.

Chapter One

Across 5 (5 letters)
The foot had the middle stolen

T HROUGH THE GLOOM, the towers of York Minster were slowly coming into view as the wipers swished rhythmically back and forth across the windscreen of the BMW travelling along the A64. From his position in the back seat, Chief Inspector John Shadow stared out of the window. He knew this sleety January rain well. It was the sort that would last all day, falling from leaden clouds that meant it would never get properly light. It wasn't much of a welcome home.

His mood wasn't improved by the fact that he seemed to have been picked up from Leeds Bradford Airport by the county's most talkative taxi driver. In his experience, Yorkshire taxi drivers usually limited themselves to a brief comment about the weather then spent the rest of the journey in silence shaking their heads and tutting at the behaviour of other road users. However, the man behind the wheel this morning had so far informed him of his wife's shortcomings when it came to making stuffing for Christmas dinner, the failings of the current Leeds United manager and the incompetence of York council's transport policy. At least Shadow hadn't been required to do more than issue the occasional nod and grunt of agreement. Until now.

"Were you in London long, mate?"

He hated being called mate.

"Only for the night."

"I don't blame you, mate. I wouldn't go to London if you paid me."

"I see."

"No. The place is full of southerners."

Shadow merely nodded again. He couldn't fault the man's logic, but he didn't feel inclined to explain that he'd only spent the night in an airport hotel after arriving at Heathrow from Bari, via Milan. He had spent Christmas and New Year in southern Italy, where Luisa, the woman he had loved and lost almost thirty years ago, had grown up. Luca, Luisa's brother, had invited Shadow to spend the festive period with him and his family. It felt a lot longer than twenty-four hours since he'd left the warmth of their hospitality and the Apulian sun behind.

The car and its talkative driver weaved through the city streets until they arrived on Skeldergate Bridge. There they pulled up by the steps that led down to the River Ouse. Shadow stepped out and looked across the dark expanse of water. He could see the outline of *Florence*, the narrow boat he had called home for nearly thirty years. However, inside right now and probably fast asleep were Jake and Missy. He'd left *Florence* in their care and didn't have the heart to wake either of them up this early. Jake and Missy, his belligerent dog, normally lived on the streets, but Shadow had let them stay aboard his barge while he was in Italy. Reluctantly, he climbed back into the taxi.

"Take me up to the Guildhall instead, will you?" he asked.

His driver shrugged. "Whatever you say. You're the one paying, mate."

The ancient medieval Guildhall had played many roles over the centuries but was now home to the city's police. Lugging his suitcase along, Shadow walked beneath the archway, across the stone-paved courtyard and through the doors into the reception. There was no sign of the desk sergeant, or anyone else. He trudged up the stairs to his office and flicked on the fluorescent light. He was relieved to see Jimmy Chang, his sergeant, had removed the artificial Christmas tree he'd insisted on putting up on Shadow's desk. Predictably though, he'd done a less than adequate job of clearing up after himself. He swept some stray strands of tinsel and glitter from his chair, took off his damp wax jacket and sat down. Various reports and memos were stacked in a pile on his desk, but Shadow ignored them. Instead, he put his feet up on the sill of the window that overlooked the river and waited for the sun to rise.

"You're back, Chief. Did you have a good time? I

thought I saw a light on in here."

Shadow woke up with a start to find his sergeant beaming at him, despite the large white foam collar around his neck.

"And your observational skills are as sharp as ever, Sergeant Chang. I suppose I should be grateful you're only in a neck brace and not on crutches," snapped back Shadow with a frown. He'd said all along that a honeymoon in the Alps was a bad idea.

"Oh, I didn't do this skiing. I slipped on some black ice getting out of the taxi home. Sophie thinks I might have whiplash and told me I should wear this for a couple of weeks. Technically, Chief, it's a cervical collar, not a neck brace."

"Is that so? And what are we busy with this morning, assuming you are capable of working in a cervical collar?"

"Of course, Chief. It does make getting in and out of cars a bit awkward though."

Shadow could well imagine. Jimmy's tall angular frame struggled to be accommodated in some of the city's low-ceilinged buildings and the smaller pool cars as it was. He stood up, stretched his shoulders and yawned.

"Then I suggest you walk to wherever you are next called out to."

"It'll be Tadcaster Road, Chief. A report of a stolen weapon has just come in," replied Jimmy, consulting his ever-present electronic notebook.

"What sort of weapon?"

"A sabre. An antique sabre to be exact. Thought to date from 1854."

"Who on earth had one of those?"

"The army, Chief."

"Oh well, that makes sense, I suppose."

"Can you give me five minutes? I need to find an umbrella. I'm not supposed to get my collar wet."

Shadow reached for his jacket hanging on the back of his chair. "Take as long as you want. I'm not going anywhere until I've had some breakfast. You know where to find me."

Five minutes later, Shadow was wiping the raindrops from his face as he took a seat at his favourite table in the corner of Bettys Tearoom. He placed his order, unfolded the copy of the *Yorkshire Post* he'd picked up at the airport and hoped his fellow diners couldn't hear his stomach growling in anticipation. There were many things he loved about Italy and the Italians, but they hadn't really got the hang of breakfast. The small piece of almond cake and cappuccino he'd had each morning didn't come close to a full English with a pot of Yorkshire tea.

As he swallowed the last mouthful of bacon and pushed his knife and fork together with a sigh of satisfaction, a massive multi-coloured umbrella appeared from the entrance to the Guildhall. Wearily he rose to his feet, paid the bill and stepped outside. He watched, bemused as Jimmy struggled to keep the umbrella steady as he skipped and dodged around puddles littering St Helen's Square. No doubt he was attempting to protect his latest pair of expensive trainers.

"I don't think much to your Gene Kelly impression," he commented.

"What's that, Chief?" his sergeant replied, looking confused.

"Never mind. Let's go."

The two of them set off, huddled together beneath the unwieldy umbrella. Shadow had to endure almost an hour of endless chatter from his sergeant, who was reporting every detail of his fortnight in the Alps as if it was a murder investigation. Shadow was only grateful he hadn't made notes. The first week, he and Sophie, his new wife and one of the pathologists they worked with, had been alone, but during the second week, they were joined by a large group of friends. Shadow heard all about who was great at skiing: Sophie. Who was useless at snowboarding: Jimmy. And who had made fools of themselves after overindulging in the après-ski: Ben and Ollie, the two forensic scientists they also worked with.

"What about you, Chief?" asked Jimmy when he'd finally finished his report. "Did you have a good time in Italy?"

"Yes, thank you."

"You've got a suntan. It really suits you. I've never seen you with a tan before."

"They aren't as easy to acquire in North Yorkshire as they are in Southern Italy."

"How was Luisa's family?"

"Fine. How did Sophie take finding out the woman who married you was a killer?"

"Actually, she took it really well. She said she was just relieved we hadn't had to rearrange the ceremony and that I should thank you for not arresting the dean until we'd left."

Shadow smiled and shook his head. Jimmy and Sophie's marriage had taken place at York Minster, and almost immediately afterwards, he'd had to arrest the dean on suspicion of murdering her husband's lover.

"Your wife might be the most pragmatic woman I've ever met. You are a lucky man."

"I am," he agreed immediately. "And like I told Soph, I bet there is an ancient proverb from the Greeks or Egyptians or someone about 'the worse the person that shall marry thee, the happier the marriage shall be.' That kind of thing."

"I hope for your sake you're right," murmured Shadow, although he wasn't convinced any culture had ever considered being married by a murderer to be a fortuitous sign. However, when it came to misplaced optimism, nobody could compete with his sergeant.

By now, they had arrived outside an impressive detached Regency villa. The large rather ugly metal gates carried a sign that read "Regiment Headquarters Yorkshire Hussars" above a crest showing a white rose over two crossed swords. Jimmy pressed the button on the intercom, and a second later a loud voice barked at them out of the tinny-sounding speaker.

"Yes, who is it? Look into the camera. Show yourselves."

Jimmy raised the umbrella, showering them both with raindrops. He and Shadow both squinted at the tiny camera.

"It's the police, sir," replied Jimmy. "Chief Inspector Shadow and Detective Sergeant Chang." He began rummaging in his pocket, but before he could produce his warrant card, the voice shouted again.

"Yes, yes. Excellent. I'll see you at the front door."

A second later, the heavy metal gate slowly opened with a loud grating sound. The two detectives walked through and up the steps leading to the polished oak front door. Neither of them needed to ring the doorbell, as it was immediately opened by a tall, grey-haired man with a neatly trimmed moustache and dressed in army fatigues. His right arm shot out, and he grasped first Shadow's hand and then Jimmy's.

"Major Ian Armitage. Good of you to come, Chief Inspector, Sergeant," he said while pumping each of their arms up and down vigorously. "Come in, come in."

"Thank you, sir," replied Shadow, stepping inside while Jimmy followed, wincing slightly and rubbing his wrist. Major Armitage's well-polished boots marched across the parquet flooring of the grand reception hall. The walls were covered in the regimental colours and huge portraits of men in dress uniform. Shadow assumed they were generals or the regiment's past colonels-in-chief.

"As I told the chap I spoke to on the phone," the major barked over his shoulder, "I'm sure it will turn up. I don't want to waste your time, but it is an offensive weapon after all and rather valuable."

"Quite right, sir," replied Shadow, quickening his pace to keep up.

The major led them through double doors into the dining room, past the vast table that, after a quick tally, Shadow noted seated thirty, and pointed to the wall above the ornate fireplace. Screwed to the wall there were four brass brackets. Two were holding an antique rifle but the other two were empty.

"That's where it should be."

"Are you able to give us a description, sir?" asked Shadow.

Major Armitage frowned for a second. "Well, it's a sabre, Chief Inspector. You know, a curved sword." He held his hands out in front of him about three feet apart. "It's about so long. Traditionally used by the cavalry. This particular one was used at the Charge of the Light Brigade."

"What was that, Major?" asked Jimmy, who was busily noting down all the details.

Shadow groaned inwardly. His sergeant's grasp of history was worse than his trainers' grip on wet surfaces. However, the major seemed to think he'd only been misheard.

"I said, it was used at the Charge of the Light Brigade," he bellowed. "Not the British army's finest hour admittedly, and of course the Russians were making a nuisance of themselves again." Shadow could see Jimmy open his mouth, so he quickly stepped in.

"When did you first become aware that the sabre was missing, sir?" he asked.

"Actually, it wasn't me who noticed it, but Stanley Beresford. He was here yesterday afternoon and called me to ask if I knew where it was. I came and had a look for myself, then telephoned you chaps."

"Stanley Beresford?" queried Jimmy.

"He's a good man, Stan. Used to be one of our sergeant majors. Retired about three years ago when his wife became ill. Now he looks after the regiment's regalia and keeps a check on our archives. He'll be the one to ask about the valuation. It made sense he was the one to spot the sabre was missing. I can tell you that it was definitely here on Saturday evening though, Chief Inspector. We had a regimental dinner. A belated celebration to commemorate the birthday of John Manners, the Marquess of Granby, our first colonel-in-chief."

"It was on view in quite a prominent position, and someone would need to stand on a stepladder to take it down. How do you think someone was able to remove it without anyone noticing, Major?" asked Shadow.

"Oh, it had already been removed from its usual position in anticipation of the dinner, Chief Inspector. Traditionally we use it to open the champagne."

"Really? That sounds amazing," said Jimmy, looking up from his notes.

"It is rather a fun party trick, Sergeant," agreed the major with an almost childish grin. "It's known as sabrage. Here let me show you." He removed his phone from one of his trouser pockets, pressed a few buttons and turned the screen towards the two detectives. Shadow fumbled to put on his reading glasses as a video began playing of a rowdy dinner consisting exclusively of men wearing the red dress uniform of the regiment. The camera scanned along the diners, then focused on the major, who was standing at the head of the table with a bottle of champagne in one hand and a sabre in the other. "The Marquess of Granby," he declared. Then with one swift motion he swung the sword down and sliced the top off the bottle. A small cloud of gas was released but barely a drop of champagne was lost. This was met by much cheering and clapping from his audience. Jimmy joined in with the applause.

"Wow. That is seriously cool," he said. "How long did it take to learn how to do it?"

"Not long at all. It's all to do with the angle and the speed. The trick is not to hesitate. I'll teach you how to do it once the sabre turns up again, Sergeant."

"Thanks! That would be amazing."

Shadow loudly cleared his throat before the two of them formed a mutual appreciation society.

"Perhaps you would be kind enough to forward that video and any other images you may have of the sabre to help with the investigation. Would I be correct in thinking the evening wasn't an entirely sober affair, sir?"

"You certainly would, Chief Inspector."

"Then could it simply be a drunken prank?" asked Shadow.

"More than likely, I'd say. That was certainly my first thought. I've sent an email out to all the chaps who were here for the dinner, but no positive responses, so I thought I should report it. It might be over a hundred and fifty years old, but you could still certainly do some damage with it. We don't want it falling into the wrong hands."

Shadow nodded and glanced around the room. There were several large windows overlooking the rear-walled garden.

"Are there any signs of a break-in?" he asked.

The major shook his head. "None whatsoever. This place is like Fort Knox. You saw for yourselves our entry system." He gestured to the garden. "There's an eight-foot wall topped with barbed wire running all the way around the place and nine times out of ten there is a serving or ex-solider on site. If you are thinking it could be some local burglar chancing his luck, then I'm sure they could find easier targets. Besides, nothing else is missing. There's a decent amount of petty cash upstairs in one of the offices and a pair of silver goblets in the hallway but nothing else has been touched."

Shadow nodded again. It was sounding more and more like it had been taken by one of the dinner guests.

"Do you recall if it was still here when you left the dining room at the end of the evening?" he asked.

"I'm afraid I can't help you there, Chief Inspector. I was completely blotto. Arthur was the only sober one amongst us."

"Arthur?" enquired Jimmy, poised to make another note.

"Our regimental whippet," replied the major. "He attends all our dinners. Wouldn't be the same without him. Although he's been a bit under the weather recently. Poor chap."

Jimmy looked impressed again. "Do all regiments have their own whippet?"

"No, we are the only ones as far as I know. The Irish Guards have an Irish wolfhound though, and the Royal Welsh have a goat and the paras have a Shetland pony. None of them are a patch on Arthur though, Sergeant."

Sensing Jimmy would be keen to know more about these regimental animal mascots, Shadow stepped forward and shook the major's hand.

"And we hope Arthur is feeling better soon. Thank you for your time, sir. If you could also email us a list of everyone who was present at the dinner and the insurance valuation of the sabre, that would be very helpful. We'll be in touch if we have any news."

"Excellent, excellent. As I said, it's bound to show up. Good day, gentlemen."

The major showed Shadow and Jimmy to the door, and

the two of them stepped back through the clanking electric gates. Fortunately, the rain had become more of a damp mist and Jimmy could now tuck the umbrella awkwardly under his arm.

"What do you think, Chief?"

"I think Major Armitage is right. The sabre will no doubt turn up in the next day or two. They were all absolutely steaming in that video. One of them will have thought it was hilarious to take it home with them and will probably return it when they discover it in their garden. Having said that, you should probably contact any auction houses or dealers in antique weapons. Check someone hasn't stolen it and is trying to sell it on. Phone around the local taxi firms too. See if anyone remembers collecting a fare from here after the dinner."

"Will do, Chief. By the way, who was this John Manners guy?" Jimmy asked as they strolled back down Tadcaster Road. "Major Armitage said they were celebrating his birthday. I thought the Marquess of Granby was the name of a pub."

"There are plenty of pubs named after him. He was the son of the Duke of Rutland and a famous general during the 1700s. He was also known for his generosity towards his men and gave retired soldiers money from his own pocket so they could set up in business as publicans."

"Wow. He sounds great. No wonder they are still celebrating him."

"Yes, not that being well-loved did him any good. He died in Scarborough before he had inherited the dukedom and was almost penniless."

By now they had now reached Blossom Street and the owner of Fryer Tuck's Fish and Chips was turning over the open sign as they approached.

"That's good timing. Let's call in here," said Shadow, sniffing the air appreciatively.

"You know it's only been a couple of hours since breakfast, Chief?"

"I am aware of the time, Sergeant. Do you have a point?"

"They don't have fish and chips in Italy, do they?"

"No, they do not," replied Shadow, rubbing his hands together as he stepped inside. "If you're not hungry, shall I just get you a dandelion and burdock?"

Jimmy pulled a face. "No thanks, I think I'll have a coffee." Then under his breath: "Actually I won't bother. I think they might only do instant."

Shadow sighed. His sergeant was something of a coffee snob.

"Please yourself. Why don't you get back to the station and start making some phone calls and leave me to eat my lunch in peace."

WHEN SHADOW EVENTUALLY arrived back at the station,

feeling a little bloated, he found Jimmy at the reception desk. He was talking to a familiar figure in camouflage trousers and jacket accompanied by a cross-looking spaniel. All three turned around when they heard him enter.

"I've brought your keys. Cheers for letting us stay," said Jake, dropping the keys to *Florence* into Shadow's hand.

"How did you know I was back?" asked Shadow.

"Good news travels fast."

"Where will you go next?" asked Jimmy, who was now on his hands and knees fussing Missy, who in return was wagging her tail in uncharacteristic delight.

"Naburn. We got talking to some other boat people down at the marina there. We're going to look after another boat that belongs to an old couple while they go off to see their grandkids in Australia. Some other weekenders want to start paying me to keep an eye on their boats too and do a bit of maintenance like."

"Hey, that's great news," replied Jimmy enthusiastically while Missy licked his face.

Jake shrugged, looking a little embarrassed. "It turns out boats suit me and Missy. And I haven't forgotten you owe me a fiver."

"Have you been gambling, Sergeant? That doesn't sound like you," said Shadow.

Jake grinned. "We had a bet. He didn't think you'd be coming back," he explained.

Now it was Jimmy's turn to look embarrassed as he got

to his feet and handed over a five-pound note.

"Well, I wasn't sure, Chief. After all, you love everything about Italy, and you seemed to really hit it off with Luca. It would have made sense if you'd decided to stay there."

Jake shook his head. "Nah, I knew you'd be back. Besides, York wouldn't be the same without your happy smiling face around the place."

He stuffed the note into his pocket and turned to go, whistling for Missy, who bounded after him through the door. Shadow watched them leave.

"I didn't know there were that many other people living on boats in York," he commented.

"Oh, there's at least a dozen or so, mainly down at Naburn, like Jake said. It's a great little community down there; you know, helping each other out and socialising." Jimmy paused. "But I guess that isn't really your kind of thing, Chief."

Shadow merely grunted in response, although it was true. He could think of little he'd like less than to be surrounded by other boats with their inhabitants forever asking to borrow something or having to constantly find excuses when they invited him to join them for a drink or, worse, supper. He chose to live on the river so he could get some peace and quiet. He already had more than enough trouble to deal with from his only neighbours: a family of delinquent geese.

"Any sign of the missing sabre?" he asked.

"No. None of the local antiques dealers or auction houses I spoke to have been approached. A couple of taxi firms reported collecting some of the officers from the regimental dinner. They confirmed everyone was pretty plastered, but nobody recalls anyone carrying anything that could have been a sabre or referring to it in any way. I'm waiting for Stanley Beresford – you know, the guy the major told us about who looks after all the regalia – to get back to me about the insurance value, but one of the auctioneers I spoke to thought it would be worth around one hundred and twenty thousand pounds. It's got excellent provenance, apparently."

Shadow raised his eyebrows. "That makes it a rather expensive bottle opener. When you speak to Mr Beresford, check who the insurance company pays out to. Is it the regiment or is an individual named on the policy?"

"Will do, Chief. What are you doing now?"

Shadow struggled to stifle a yawn. "I'm going upstairs to catch up on some paperwork."

Jimmy grinned. "Good idea, Chief. By the way, there's some cushions and pillows in the well-being room if you need them."

"The what?" asked Shadow with a frown.

"The well-being room. It's in George's old office next to the archives. The chief constable came up with the idea while you were away. She thought it would be good to have a place for any officers who are feeling stressed to go and chill out for a bit. There's blackout blinds and dim lighting, sofas, blankets and a sound system that plays relaxing music. It's really popular."

Shadow turned away, shaking his head. "Good, and I'm sure it will boost conviction rates too. No criminal wants to face the prospect of a chilled-out police officer arresting them."

He returned to his office, still grumbling to himself, and resumed his previous position of sitting in his chair with his feet on the windowsill. It was more than adequate. Why anyone should need sofas and blankets when they were meant to be working, he'd never know. He picked up the pile of papers on his desk and dropped them into the rubbish bin. The suitcase, still in the corner where he'd left it, reminded him that he should probably return to *Florence* and unpack. There was no excuse now Jake had returned the keys, but for some reason the idea didn't appeal. Instead, he turned his attention to the remaining clues in his crossword.

It was several hours later when he was woken again with a start by the sound of his office door opening and his sergeant's cheerful greeting.

"Why do I feel like I'm experiencing déjà vu?" he complained.

"Sorry, Chief, but it's five o'clock."

"I must have dozed off. It's probably jet lag."

"I told Mum you're back. She wants you to come to supper tonight."

Shadow stood up, feeling slightly mollified. "That's very

kind of her."

"She knew you wouldn't have been shopping yet, and I was telling her about the food you'd missed out on in Italy. I think she assumed that would include her beef in black bean sauce."

"She was right on both counts. Any more news about the missing sabre?"

"Stanley Beresford called me back and confirmed that it is insured for one hundred and thirty thousand pounds."

"Did he say who would get the money?"

"An individual isn't named on the policy, so it would ultimately go to the Ministry of Defence, but Mr Beresford thinks there is a chance the insurance company might not pay out if it turns out it has been lost after being taken out of the regimental headquarters by a serving officer without permission."

"So, if it doesn't turn up, it could prove to be quite embarrassing for the major. He didn't seem particularly concerned though, did he?"

"No," agreed Jimmy. "But like he said, it was probably only a prank, and it will be returned. Mr Beresford also mentioned that some of the regiment, including quite a few who were at the dinner, are now away on manoeuvres up in Scotland. They might not have received the major's email. He emailed me a decent photo of the sabre, so I've circulated that too."

"Then, I don't see there's much more we can do right

now. Time to go."

The two of them left the station and walked across St Helen's Square and down Stonegate. Even in January, it was busy with shoppers laden down with bags after a successful hunting trip for a bargain in the sales. It had grown dark whilst Shadow had been dozing, but at least the rain had stopped for a while. As they passed the Minster, the bells chimed a quarter past the hour.

"We're early," commented Shadow, knowing the Golden Dragon didn't usually open until six.

"I'm going to the theatre tonight so Mum said she would cook for us before the restaurant opens."

"What are you going to see?"

"*Snow White* – it's this year's pantomime from the Ebor Entertainers. Apparently, they always hand out tickets to the police, the hospital, the fire service. It was the chief constable's idea that I go and represent the station – you know, as a kind of reward for helping catch the Snowman," he explained, referring to a gangster who had recently been apprehended.

Shadow grunted and shook his head. "They do say no good deed goes unpunished."

"What's wrong with pantomimes?"

"They are the worst contribution this country has made to the world of so-called entertainment…" he paused "…with the possible of exception of Morris dancing."

Jimmy shrugged. "I'm really looking forward to it. I've

never been to a pantomime before."

"Then think yourself lucky."

Just then, Shadow spotted a petite woman wrapped up in her favourite green coat, hat and scarf hurrying towards them from the other end of Goodramgate. He raised his hand in greeting.

"Hello, stranger," said Maggie. "How's the neck, Jimmy?"

"Not too bad, thank you, Mrs Jackson."

She turned back to Shadow. "How was Italy? You don't look very happy to be back."

"That's my fault," replied Jimmy before Shadow could say a word. "I mentioned pantomimes, and it turns out he's not a fan."

"She knows that already. Our primary school used to make us go every year," complained Shadow.

"I think it was meant to be a treat, not a trial, John," said Maggie and grinned at Jimmy. "Even when he was eight years old, he would sit there in the stalls with his arms folded and a face like thunder. Ignore him, love. You'll have a great time."

"Thanks, I hope so, but I don't really like the idea of going on my own."

"Oh no, that will be a bit lonely," agreed Maggie. She gave Shadow a meaningful look.

"Why aren't you taking Sophie?" he asked quickly.

"She's working."

"What about your mum or your sister?"

"Mum's working as well and Angela will already be there. She's helping out backstage. Some of her pupils are playing the seven dwarves. That only leaves Grandad, and it would be no good taking him. You know what his English is like. He'll never work out what's going on."

"He won't be the only one. It'll be utter nonsense," chuntered Shadow.

"For goodness' sake," chided Maggie. "Stop trying to get out of it. A night out won't kill you. Who knows, a miracle might happen and you might actually enjoy yourself."

"Why don't you go with him, if you're so keen?" he shot back defensively.

"I'm already going. I got my great-nieces and nephews tickets for Christmas, so my sister and I are taking them tomorrow night before I go away."

"Where are you going?"

"Spain." She gave an exaggerated shiver. "I'm in serious need of some winter sun, plus Sam didn't come home for Christmas and New Year, so I'm going over to celebrate his birthday with him instead."

Shadow let this news sink in for a second, surprised by how disappointed he felt.

"How long are you going for?" he asked.

Maggie shrugged. "I'm not sure. I haven't booked a return ticket yet. Why?"

"I was just making conversation."

"Well, that's a first!"

"We're going for dinner with Mum. Would you like to join us?" asked Jimmy.

"Maybe another time, love. I need to get to the post office before it closes. Enjoy your evening. Both of you."

And with that she walked briskly down the street, waving to various other shopkeepers and people she knew. Shadow watched her go before striding after Jimmy.

"Did she seem a bit tetchy to you?" he asked.

Jimmy frowned. "Not really. Well, maybe she wasn't quite as chatty as usual. Have you done something to upset her?"

"How could I? I've only been back five minutes."

Jimmy gave him a sidelong look. "You know, you might get back into her good books if she thinks you followed her suggestion and came to the pantomime tonight."

Shadow held up his hand in surrender. "All right, all right. Anything for a quiet life."

They arrived at the Golden Dragon, Jimmy's mother's restaurant, and Rose rushed to greet her son as if she hadn't seen him for a year. Then she politely shook Shadow's hand and welcomed him home before ushering them to their usual table next to the kitchen.

"You look so thin, Jimmy! Let me get you some spring rolls and prawn toast," she called over her shoulder as she disappeared into the kitchen.

"When did you last see her?" whispered Shadow.

"Last week," Jimmy whispered back. "I don't think she's got used to me not living at home yet. She thinks I'm not eating enough and nearly burst into tears when she saw what had happened to my neck."

At that moment, Jimmy's grandfather came down the stairs. The old man gave Shadow a toothy grin and pointed to Jimmy. "He's behind you! Ha! Ha!" before continuing on his way into the kitchen still chuckling.

"What happened to him not speaking any English?" asked Shadow.

"Angela has been teaching him some of the audience participation bits from the pantomime. He loves it."

"Like I said, you should take him," muttered Shadow. The grandfather appeared again, this time with his backgammon board tucked under his arm.

"Time for a game?" asked Shadow. The two of them always played when he visited.

"Oh no it isn't!" replied the old man with another grin as he placed the pieces on the board. Shadow sighed. He'd preferred it when he was silent.

Chapter Two

Across 2 (9 letters)
Emma flies into Peru capital for this festive farce

THE MEAL AS usual was delicious but over far too quickly for Shadow's liking, and by half past six, Jimmy was practically pushing him out the door.

"What's the rush?" he grumbled as he turned up the collar of his jacket. "You said it doesn't start until half past seven."

"If we get there early, we might be able to go backstage."

"What on earth for?"

"Oh, you know, to soak up the atmosphere, and I might be able to get some autographs."

"I thought you said it was an amateur production."

"It is, but you never know, one of the cast could go on to be famous. Angela said the girl who plays Snow White is really good. She's going to drama school down in London in September. She could be the next big thing."

Shadow shook his head. It was clear nothing was going to dampen his sergeant's enthusiasm for the evening's events. They arrived at York's Theatre Royal a few minutes later.

The huge Gothic building dominated St Leonard's Place and had been entertaining the city's residents and visitors since 1744. They entered the foyer that unlike the outside of the building was a modern mix of glass and chrome with the occasional piece of exposed stone wall. The place was practically deserted apart from a very smiley young lady who sold them both a programme.

"I told you we'd be too early," griped Shadow as he wondered which way the bar was. Jimmy nudged him in the ribs and pointed to a short, fat, balding man with huge glasses hurrying through the door.

"Look! It's 'with you 'til ten Len'!"

"Who?"

"With you 'til ten Len. Len Horning from *Horning in the Morning*. He's playing the dame." Shadow still stared back blankly at his sergeant's excited grin. "The breakfast show on the local radio station. You must have listened to it, Chief. He's an institution."

"It looks like he belongs in one," muttered Shadow. The man Jimmy was so impressed with was wearing a headache-inducing combination of bright yellow trousers with a lurid green shirt and orange waistcoat.

"I'm going to see if I can get him to sign my programme," said Jimmy before dashing after the rotund man, leaving Shadow alone. For a second, he considered escaping, but then he reasoned he'd never hear the end of it from Maggie. With a sense of resignation, he made his way upstairs to the bar and ordered a large gin and tonic. He stared out of the window and down to the road below. The cars queuing at the traffic lights had switched their windscreen wipers on. Flakes of sleety snow were beginning to fall and flashed in the beams of their headlights.

He watched as other members of the audience began to arrive, all muffled up against the freezing weather. Then he groaned inwardly as he noticed a man of about his age appear in the doorway of the bar and remove the black hat and cloak he was wearing with a dramatic flourish, then pause as if expecting a round of applause. Malcolm Webster had been a suspect in several previous investigations before becoming something of a reformed character since beginning a relationship with the chief constable's sister. However, that didn't stop him being one of the most irritating people Shadow had ever met. He put his head down and stepped behind a nearby chrome pillar, but not quick enough.

"Ah ha, Chief Inspector Shadow! I had no idea you were a lover of the arts." Malcolm appeared in front of him looking very pleased with himself.

"I'm only here to represent the police station," replied Shadow.

"Yes, of course, just our little way of thanking the heroes in our community."

"Our little way?"

"The Ebor Entertainers. The company responsible for tonight's extravaganza. Strictly speaking, I shouldn't include myself, as they are a company of amateurs, whereas I trained professionally at RADA, but I thought it only fair to share my knowledge and experience."

"You're in the pantomime?" asked Shadow, wondering if the night could get any worse.

"I am the director!" he declared, enunciating every syllable of the last word, then he leant towards Shadow and raising his hand whispered conspiratorially, "And between you and me they need all the help they can get. Now you must excuse me. There's only thirty minutes until the curtain goes up."

And with that he disappeared, blowing kisses to the bar staff as he went. Shadow took another large glug of his G&T. The place was starting to fill up with grandparents, parents and their overexcited children. Realising he didn't have a ticket and that he was unlikely to be admitted into the auditorium without one, Shadow knocked back the last of his drink and decided it was time to go in search of his missing sergeant. He skirted round the queue that was forming at the bar and opened the door Malcolm Webster had disappeared through. He headed down a long corridor then up a flight of stairs until he found another door marked "backstage". He opened it to reveal a scene of chaos. People were hurrying back and forth amongst the wicker baskets full of props and costumes, shouting to each other.

Shadow carefully stepped around a pile of plastic picks and axes but was nearly knocked off his feet by a tall, skinny young man who came charging out of one of the small dressing rooms.

"Sorry, sorry," he apologised immediately, lifting his tricorn hat. The next second, Angela – Jimmy's sister – opened another door.

"Angela, have you seen my script anywhere?" asked the young man.

"Yes, you left it in the bar," she replied. The young man immediately turned and headed towards the door Shadow had just entered through. "Don't let Malcolm catch you wearing your costume in public before the performance. Remember, we mustn't shatter the illusion," Angela called after him, then grinned at Shadow. "I don't know why he's bothering with a script. He doesn't have any lines. I didn't know you were home, Chief Inspector. It's good to see you."

Before he could reply, a tall, well-built blond man came striding towards them. He completely ignored Shadow but flashed Angela a smile.

"No opening-night nerves, I hope, Angie. Break a leg," he said with a wink.

Angela nodded politely and murmured, "You too," then rolled her eyes as soon as he had passed by. "That's Spencer Knight, our leading man. He thinks he's God's gift," she hissed. "I didn't know you were coming to watch us tonight, Chief Inspector. I wouldn't have thought a pantomime was really your thing."

"And you would have been right. You haven't seen your

brother, have you?"

Angela frowned and shook her head. "He was here five minutes ago, but I don't know where he went. Sorry, I can't help you find him. I need to make sure all the dwarves have been to the loo before the curtain goes up." And with that she disappeared back into the dressing room.

Alone again, Shadow cursed Jimmy for about the tenth time that night. Outside the dressing room at the far end of the corridor, he watched the blond man who had winked at Angela. He was now whispering into the ear of an exceptionally pretty dark-haired young woman. Shadow squinted. She couldn't have been more than eighteen, less than half Spencer Knight's age at least. However, unlike Angela, this girl seemed enchanted by his attention. She was staring up at him with wide eyes and a shy smile on her lips.

"And that's our leading lady, Lottie Beresford," said Angela, who had reappeared, holding on to a dwarf with each hand. "Snow White and her Prince Charming. Rather her than me," she continued as she shepherded her charges through the door marked WC. At that moment, Jimmy appeared through the door that led back to the bar.

"Chief, there you are! I thought you'd ditched me."

"No such luck," grumbled Shadow as he followed his sergeant out to the auditorium.

"Look, we've got great seats," enthused Jimmy as an usher tore their tickets and directed them down the centre aisle. Shadow couldn't agree. They were far too close to the stage and to the group of six small children who were already jumping up and down in their seats. He watched as Malcolm made his way to a seat on the front row, waving and making sure as many people could see him as possible. Shadow took his own seat and checked at his watch. It was half past seven. *In two hours, it will all be over,* he reassured himself. He twisted his head around to look up at the dress circle and upper circle. The place was almost full. He consulted his programme. It informed him that the theatre could seat almost seven hundred and fifty people. When it came to pantomimes, it seemed he was in a minority after all.

As he looked up again, he saw a tall grey-haired man making his way down to the last seat in the row in front of him. It was Major Armitage. Shadow frowned. He couldn't imagine a pantomime was his preferred choice of an evening's entertainment, and by the look of things he was alone. There was no sign of a wife or any children. He was about to mention the major's presence to Jimmy, but at that moment, the lights dimmed, the music began to play and Shadow felt his heart sink. As a pantomime horse came prancing on to the stage, he gave a quiet groan and closed his eyes. But it was no good, he would never be able to sleep through all the noise, especially not now the small child sitting behind him had started kicking the back of his seat. Reluctantly, he opened his eyes again. The dame was now onstage wearing a ridiculous costume of green and purple, along with an even more preposterous orange wig. He would have felt sorry for

Mr Horning if he hadn't witnessed how he dressed when he wasn't onstage.

Next, the seven dwarves appeared followed by Snow White, who immediately broke into song. The dame encouraged the audience to join in the chorus and Jimmy was one of the first to loudly oblige. Tutting quietly to himself, Shadow turned his attention back to the programme. He flicked through until he found the cast list. Snow White, who seemed to be the only person in the place who could sing in tune, was played by Lottie Beresford, the young lady he'd seen backstage. According to her biography she had won a place at LAMDA. She must be the budding star Jimmy had mentioned. Beneath the information about Lottie was a photo of Spencer Knight, the man he had seen her talking to and who was playing Prince Charming. Shadow grunted quietly to himself. He would have thought he was a bit old to play the part himself, but the man in question had now appeared onstage and judging by the giggles and the looks exchanged by the two mothers on the row in front of him, he could be wrong.

He stopped reading and thought for a second. Beresford. Wasn't that the name of the man who had first noticed the sabre was missing? Suddenly, his sergeant gave his arm a sharp jab with his elbow, interrupting his thoughts.

"Look," hissed Jimmy. "It's Angela! The evil queen can't have turned up. She's the understudy."

Shadow looked up at the stage and squinted. It was true.

The figure dressed in black and red satin and wearing a glistening crown was indeed his sergeant's sister. Her evil cackle was met by much booing and hissing. Shadow's first thought was who would be looking after the dwarves now if Angela was onstage, and his second was who hadn't turned up? The programme informed him that the evil queen should have been played by a someone called Francesca French. The accompanying black and white photo showed a glamorous brunette who seemed to be simultaneously pouting and sucking her cheeks in for the camera. She looked to be in her early forties. A good twenty years older than her understudy.

He watched Angela explain her wicked plan to rid herself of Snow White to her henchman, who was played by Rohan Kapoor, the clumsy young man in the tricorn hat he'd almost bumped into backstage. He had to admit the normally caring and polite schoolteacher was quite frighteningly convincing. After another cackle she disappeared in a cloud of smoke, the curtain closed, and to his relief it was time for the interval.

"What do you think so far, Chief?" asked Jimmy as soon as the lights went up.

"I think you should move very quickly if you want to get to the bar and back before the second half begins."

Jimmy obediently did as he was told. Shadow waited until the predictable stampede for the toilets, bar and ice cream vendor had subsided, then he rose to his feet, stretched and yawned. The theatre seating might have improved since he was a child, but he wasn't sure – forty years later – his back could handle another hour sat there. He was seriously considering making his escape when Jimmy suddenly reappeared proudly carrying a large plastic glass of red wine aloft.

"How did you get served so quickly?" asked Shadow.

Jimmy grinned. "Tom is helping out in the stalls bar. He knew I was bringing you, so he had a glass of Chianti ready and waiting. We reckoned it was the only thing that might stop you doing a runner."

"I've never done a runner in my life," retorted Shadow, sniffing suspiciously at the wine. He took a sip. Despite being served in a half-pint plastic tumbler, it actually didn't taste too bad. "And if Tom's here anyway, I don't know why you couldn't make him watch this with you."

"He's meant to be videoing the production up in the gods with the sound and lighting team. He's only helping out in the bar because they are short-staffed."

Shadow nodded. Tom was a constable who had recently taken over the role of maintaining the archives at the station. He also happened to be going out with Jimmy's sister.

"Angela didn't mention she would be performing. Did she get much warning that she would be going on?" he asked.

"None. Apparently Francesca, who normally plays the role, is a bit of a diva. She just didn't turn up. No phone call.

Nothing. I think Ange is doing okay though, don't you?"

"I think she and Snow White are the only ones holding the whole thing together," muttered Shadow. "Who is looking after the dwarves while she's onstage?"

"Tom said two other members of the cast have got DBS clearance, so they're helping out."

Shadow nodded as he reluctantly folded himself back into the flip-up seat. As he awkwardly shifted his knees from side to side to allow those in the neighbouring seats to pass by, he noticed that Major Armitage had yet to return. He kept watching his seat, but it remained empty. Taking another sip of wine, he couldn't help feeling a little envious that the other man had managed to escape. The lights dimmed and the audience began shushing each other. The last to return to his seat was Malcolm, who tiptoed through the darkness in a typically exaggerated manner.

Shadow had hoped the large glass of wine might help him snooze during the second half, but the audience, now fuelled by either alcohol or sugar depending on their age, had lost any inhibitions they may have had about taking part in the performance. They began hissing and booing enthusiastically as the evil queen appeared onstage. Above the cacophony, she managed to explain that she was going to poison Prince Charming before he could propose to Snow White, then left a bottle of green liquid on an unconvincing toadstool before sneaking away and hiding behind an equally unrealistic cardboard tree.

A second later, Prince Charming appeared, and Shadow almost fell off his seat as Jimmy yelled out, "She's behind you!" at the top of his voice. Was it his imagination or was Angela shaking her head? The prince picked up the bottle she'd left behind.

"What's this?" he asked. "On the label it says, 'love potion'. Shall I drink it, boys and girls?"

Shadow winced as everyone began screaming "No!" Naturally, the prince chose to ignore them.

"If I drink this, Snow White is sure to marry me," he said with a wink and then knocked back the bright green liquid and promptly fell to the floor. Before the evil queen could make her move, the dame came running back on to the stage wearing an even more ludicrous outfit than the last.

"He's been poisoned!" screeched the audience.

"Poisoned, you say? Then it's my lucky day! I'll give him the kiss of life!"

Shadow rolled his eyes as the dame made a great show of applying more lipstick and puckering up before swooping down to plant a kiss on the prince's lips. This sent everyone into fits of laughter. Everyone except Shadow, who was now focused on the dame's face. The smile had disappeared and there was a look in Len Horning's eyes that worried him. The dame gave the prince, who still hadn't moved, a shake.

"Come on now, Your Highness. Wakey-wakey!"

It was clear Len was trying to stay in character but there was a note of panic in his voice. Angela must have heard it too, as she left her hiding place behind the tree and hurried forward accompanied by much booing from the oblivious audience. She bent down and took hold of the prince's wrist then signalled frantically to the someone offstage. A second later, the heavy red velvet curtains swished closed. The audience fell silent, then Angela's head appeared through the gap in the curtains.

"Is there a doctor in the house?" she called out, then shading her eyes against the bright lights: "Jimmy? Chief Inspector? Where are you? Please come quickly."

The two detectives were already out of their seats and pushing their way past the rest of their row. The audience had begun murmuring, and at least two children had started sobbing as Shadow and Jimmy hurried on to the stage and ducked behind the curtain after Angela. Malcolm had followed them too.

"Why did you break the fourth wall, Angela?" he demanded.

"He's not breathing, and I can't feel a pulse," she whispered. By now, most of the cast were onstage and crowded around the motionless prince. Angela quickly rounded up the dwarves and ushered them away. Jimmy dropped to his knees and started checking for signs of life, but almost immediately looked up at Shadow and shook his head.

"I'm going to try CPR, Chief. Maybe he's had a heart attack," he said and, with the help of Len, turned the prince over and began chest compressions while Shadow called an ambulance. As he finished the call, Snow White began sobbing. An older man, dressed in black, put his arm around her shoulder and tried to comfort her. While everyone else's eyes were on Jimmy, Shadow knelt down and carefully retrieved the empty glass bottle from where it had rolled beneath the toadstool. Despite his sergeant's best efforts, he didn't think Spencer Knight had suffered a heart attack, and he didn't think there was any chance of him being resuscitated. He carefully slipped the empty bottle into his pocket, then placed his hand on Jimmy's shoulder. His sergeant stopped pummelling the dead man's chest and looked up.

"It's been nearly ten minutes. Leave him be now," Shadow said gently. Jimmy's face fell, but he nodded his head in resignation. Snow White began sobbing even more loudly and Len had turned pale beneath his thick make-up.

"Could you please all return to your dressing rooms and stay there. We'll come and speak to you as soon as we can," said Shadow.

"What about the children?" called Angela from the wings, her voice still shaking. "Can they go home?"

"Yes," he replied, "contact their parents and ask them to come and collect them. We'll arrange to speak to them later if necessary."

He waited until the cast had reluctantly shuffled offstage, then he stepped out on to the stage. The lights of the auditorium were on but so were the footlights and he had to shield his eyes from the glare.

"Ladies and gentlemen, my name is Chief Inspector Shadow," he began, and the restless audience fell silent. "I'm sorry to inform you that the rest of this evening's performance has been cancelled. I should be grateful if you would leave the theatre as quietly and calmly as possible."

"What about our tickets?" shouted someone he couldn't see.

"Will we get a refund?" asked a voice nearer the stage.

"Why's it been cancelled?" called out another anonymous audience member.

"What's happened to Prince Charming, Chief Inspector?" asked another with a slight Scottish accent, which Shadow recognised immediately. It was Kevin MacNab, a journalist from the local newspaper and one of his least favourite people. That's all he needed: the press sticking their noses in. Shadow held up his hand to silence the increasing swell of voices.

"I'm sure the box office will be happy to answer your questions. Thank you." And with that he quickly stepped back behind the curtain. Jimmy had been joined by Tom. They were both on their mobiles calling for assistance. Shadow stared down at Spencer Knight's handsome, lifeless face. His blue eyes were staring up at him, and he had to resist the urge to close them. Sophie wouldn't want him to be touched. Tom was the first to finish his call.

"What can you tell us about him?" asked Shadow.

Tom shrugged. "Not much, Chief. I only spoke to him a

couple of times. His name was Spencer Knight. He had his own business and was a bit of a ladies' man by all accounts. I think he and Lottie, the girl playing Snow White, were having a bit of thing."

"Wasn't she a little young for him?"

"Maybe, but Angela also said the two of them were pretty close," replied Jimmy, who had finished his call as well.

"Do you know if he'd complained of feeling unwell?" Shadow asked Tom.

"I don't think so. He seemed liked a pretty fit guy. He played golf and tennis and went swimming a lot. He was a member of that flash new gym that opened near the university and the North York Golf Club."

"Do you think it was natural causes, Chief?" asked Jimmy. Shadow shook his head and removed the small glass bottle from his pocket.

"I don't know. But I do know he collapsed after drinking whatever was in here."

He unscrewed the top and sniffed. There was a faint whiff of citrus fruits.

"It's only meant to be lime cordial with some green food colouring in it," explained Tom.

"Chief, you really shouldn't be touching that without gloves on," said Jimmy as he produced an evidence bag from somewhere inside his leather jacket.

"Do you always carry one of those?" asked Tom.

"Yep. Usually. Sophie laughs at me, but you never know

when they might come in handy. Like now. Don't look like that. It's important to follow procedure."

"Says the man who interfered with the body," huffed Shadow as he dropped the bottle into the small plastic bag Jimmy was holding open.

"I was trying to save his life," protested Jimmy.

Shadow grunted and turned his attention back to Tom.

"Do we know who his next of kin is? Was he married? Children?"

"No," replied Tom, "I never heard him talk about any family. Francesca is his business partner. She was meant to be playing the evil queen, but she didn't show up tonight. Malcolm and Angela both tried calling but nobody has heard from her."

"All right. You stay here with the body and try contacting her again. We'll go and have a look in his dressing room."

Shadow and Jimmy stepped backstage for the second time that evening. The atmosphere had completely changed. It was empty, all the dressing-room doors were shut, and the only sounds were hushed conversations and muffled sobbing. Spencer Knight's dressing room was almost at the end of the corridor and the door was unlocked. The two detectives stepped inside. Shadow looked around the small space. There was a table and chair in front of a mirror surrounded by lights, a washbasin in the corner and a metal rail where Spencer's clothes were hanging. Jimmy began searching through his jacket pockets.

"He left his phone and wallet here." He opened the leather wallet. "There are three credit cards, all platinum, and at least a couple of hundred in cash. He must have thought it was safe to leave stuff in here without needing to lock the door. His phone's here too, but it's locked."

"See if forensics can get into it. Anything else?"

Jimmy removed the driving licence and a business card from the wallet and began reading. "Spencer Knight, forty-two years old, lived at an address on Bishopthorpe Road. He had his own business, Knight and French Associates."

"And what did Knight and French Associates do?"

"It says here, financial advisers."

"That covers a multitude of sins. Any mention of who his next of kin might be?"

"His contact in case of an emergency person is Francesca French, his business partner."

"Maybe not just his business partner then," mused Shadow. "Check his trouser pockets too. Any sign of tablets or medication of any sort?"

Jimmy began rummaging again but shook his head. At that moment, there was a quick knock and Tom put his head around the door.

"Sorry to interrupt, Chief, but Sophie and forensics are here."

When they arrived back onstage, they found Sophie kneeling next to the corpse. She looked up when she heard them. "Welcome home, Chief. Hi, Jimmy," she said and shook her head. "Only you two could go the pantomime and end the evening with a dead body."

"Evening, Sophie," said Shadow. "He collapsed after drinking this." He gestured to Jimmy, who produced the glass bottle in the plastic bag and handed it to his wife. "But it could be natural causes. Any thoughts?"

Sophie took the evidence bag and frowned. "It's hard to say, Chief. There is a slight blue tinge to his lips and nails and his pupils are slightly dilated, which could indicate poisoning, but I won't know until I have analysed this and examined him properly."

Shadow nodded but before he could reply, Jimmy stepped in.

"Hey, Soph, guess what? He lived on Bishopthorpe Road."

She looked up with interest. "Really?"

"Why is that significant?" asked Shadow with a frown.

Jimmy looked a little embarrassed. "It isn't for the case, Chief, but we've been thinking about trying to buy a place and Bishopthorpe Road is one of our favourite areas. I know it isn't very sensitive, but, well, it might mean that this guy's place will be coming on the market and—"

"Houses there are like gold dust," completed Sophie.

"Popular area, is it?" asked Shadow, who, living on a boat, had never had much interest in the city's property market.

"Very," she replied. "Jimmy wants us to hang out with all the hipsters."

"Hipsters? Didn't they used to be called yuppies?"

"Not in this century, Chief," Sophie said with a laugh.

"Are you saying I'm getting old, Sophie?"

"No, not you, Chief. You were born old."

Shadow couldn't really argue, and besides he was distracted by a commotion coming from behind the curtain. He had to stifle a groan as Ben and Ollie appeared through the red velvet. At the best of times, he found the two forensic scientists exasperating, but today the two of them were approaching him with matching grins and neck braces identical to Jimmy's.

"Chief! You're back!" they chorused.

"Don't tell me you two slipped getting out of a taxi too?"

"No, we fell off the chairlift when we were trying to take a selfie," explained Ben.

"What have we got?" asked Ollie.

"We think he might have been poisoned," replied Sophie.

"Oh no he hasn't!" joked Ben, sending Ollie into peals of laughter.

"Hey, Ben. Where's Jimmy?"

"He's behind you!"

"For crying out loud!" exclaimed Shadow, the last of his patience having evaporated. "Can you at least try to be professional for once?"

"Come on, Chief. We're at the pantomime," replied Ben. "It's only a bit of fun."

"It could also be a crime scene. It's bad enough that you look like the Three Stooges. Do I have to remind you that a man is dead? Show some respect."

"Sorry, Chief," replied the two scientists in unison again. Shadow turned away, shaking his head. Out of the corner of his eye, he saw Jimmy mouthing "Who are the Three Stooges?" to Sophie, but his wife merely smiled and shook her head again.

Shadow sighed. "Come on, Sergeant Chang. Let's go and speak to some of the cast."

"Who do you want to speak to first, Chief?"

"Under normal circumstances, I would have said the last person to handle the bottle before Knight drank from it, but as that was your sister, let's start with our pantomime dame. What did you say his name was? Len something?"

"Horning, Chief. Len Horning."

Shadow knocked on the door bearing the dame's real name and his heart sank when he stepped inside to find Len was not alone, but sharing a bottle of gin with the director, Malcolm Webster.

"Ah, Chief Inspector Shadow and Sergeant Chang, allow me to introduce my partner in crime, Len Horning. The two of us created the Ebor Entertainers ten fun-filled years ago."

"Drink, officers?" offered Len. He'd removed his wig but was still in costume and full make-up and was refilling the chipped ceramic mugs he and Malcolm were drinking from.

Shadow shook his head. "No thank you, Mr Horning," he replied.

Malcolm raised a finger to his lips. "Not a word to Harriet. She's away at a conference, but she thinks I've knocked the bottle on the head, so to speak."

Shadow wasn't remotely concerned if Malcolm had given up being teetotal and returned to his old ways, but he was struck by the fact that neither man seemed particularly upset by the sudden death of their co-star.

As if reading his mind, Malcolm put down his mug and cleared his throat.

"So, Chief Inspector, are you able to tell us what happened to poor Spencer? Terrible thing to occur and on opening night too. Did his heart give out or do you suspect foul play?"

"We are still trying ascertain the cause of Mr Knight's death, but we would like to ask you a few questions."

"Chief Inspector, if I may, I should like to anticipate your first question. Did he have any enemies?" asked Malcolm.

"And did he?" replied Shadow. He had actually been going to enquire about the dead man's health, but he decided to play along.

Malcolm looked at Len and grinned. "Well, where do I start?" began Malcolm.

"Spurned lovers!" suggested Len.

"Cuckolded husbands!" added Malcolm.

"Jealous admirers!" Len again.

"Cheated clients!" And back to Malcolm.

Shadow thought it was a pity they hadn't chosen to put on *Cinderella* instead of *Snow White*. Malcolm and Len would have been the perfect double act to play the ugly stepsisters.

"So would you say Mr Knight was a 'ladies' man'?" asked Jimmy, his notebook poised ready.

Len reached over and gave him an affectionate pat on the arm.

"Now, that is the understatement of the year, Sergeant Chang!"

"I heard he was in a relationship with the girl playing Snow White," said Shadow.

"Darling Lottie! The star of our show, but you could hardly call it a relationship, Chief Inspector. More of an infatuation," replied Malcolm.

"But on whose part?" added Len, arching his heavily pencilled eyebrow.

"Angela Chang was covering for someone who didn't turn up tonight," Shadow pressed on.

"Oh, what a trouper the lovely Angela has been! As well as keeping an eye on all the kiddies, she offered to be the understudy for Snow White and the evil queen. She'd been here for all the rehearsals, so she knew the script by heart," explained Malcolm.

"Which is more than you could say for Francesca," added Len.

"Francesca French, who should have been playing the part of the evil queen?" asked Shadow.

Len huffed dramatically and rolled his eyes. "It wouldn't surprise me if she didn't turn up on purpose. She'd been spitting feathers ever since Malcolm told her she was too old to play Snow White. He was quite right of course. She was forty if she was a day. I told her straight. 'Even the best make-up artist can't work miracles, love, and no matter how good the lighting is nobody is going to believe you are a winsome teenager.' Oh, she looked like a bulldog chewing a wasp!"

"Do you know where we can find Miss French or is it Mrs French?"

"I believe she prefers Ms and the person to ask would have been Spencer. They were partners in business as well as other things if the gossip is to be believed."

"Did they live together?"

"Nooo!" replied Len, shaking his head vigorously. "Not that I don't think she would have leapt at the chance if he'd asked her. But moving in with someone, that was a bit too much like commitment for our Spencer. What if someone better came along? Although, I think she was trying to get him to invest in a cottage with her. They were meant to be doing it up to sell on, but I think she thought she'd wear him down over time. Patience of a spider that one!"

"What about the rest of the cast?" asked Shadow as Jimmy tapped away at his notebook.

"Well," said Malcolm, "the pantomime horse was Steven West at the front and Matthew West at the rear, so to speak."

Shadow frowned. He'd come across those names during a previous investigation.

"The two brothers who run a ghost-walking business from above a shop on Shambles?" he asked.

"Cousins actually, Chief," supplied Jimmy, earning himself a scowl. It was bad enough trying to keep track of what Len and Malcolm were telling him without his sergeant complicating things with unnecessary details.

"And if you have ever had the misfortune to experience one of their walks and their thespian skills – or lack of them – then you will know exactly why I made sure they were hidden away inside Dobbin," said Malcolm waspishly.

"Even so, I would like to speak to them."

"Oh, you can't, I'm afraid. They went to the pub. The Guy Fawkes Inn, I believe. Said they needed a drink to steady their nerves. I told them it would be fine."

"I did ask all adults involved in the production to remain here at the theatre," replied Shadow, unable to keep the irritation out of his voice.

"But why?" protested Len. "We still don't know what happened to Spencer, and if it was foul play, it couldn't possibly be Steve or Matt. They are literally sewn into that costume and don't come out until the final curtain call."

"You mean they are dressed as the pantomime horse for nearly three hours?" asked Jimmy incredulously.

"Quite, Sergeant Chang. It's Matt I feel particularly sorry for. Apparently, the key is not to drink anything for at least an hour before the performance. It gets very warm in old Dobbin; the poor souls come out quite dehydrated," explained Len, sloshing more gin into the two mugs.

"Hence the need for liberal libation," added Malcolm.

"I see," interrupted Shadow, keen to get the line of questioning back on track. "Who else is there we can speak to?"

"Let me see. Derek and Diane Dawson are responsible for sound and lighting, but they are up their control centre in the gods and never come backstage. Susan is in charge of costumes and props. Stan Beresford helps us out backstage, moving scenery – that sort of thing. In truth, I think he likes being here to keep an eye on Lottie. She's his pride and joy."

"Even more so since he lost poor Ann," added Len. "God rest her."

"Oh, and there's Rohan Kapoor, our evil henchman," continued Malcolm.

"Now if anyone was ever cast against type," chuckled Len, shaking his head. "Such a sweet boy."

"No acting background whatsoever and so uncoordinated, but darling Lottie brought him to rehearsals once and he sort of stuck around. I believe he's helping Angela with the little ones now, Chief Inspector."

"I see, thank you. Now were either of you aware of any health issues Mr Knight may have had?"

"Spencer!" exclaimed Len. "No, not him. He was as fit as a fiddle. He certainly got plenty of exercise." He gave Jimmy an exaggerated wink. "If you know what I mean."

"Due to being a ladies' man?" asked Jimmy.

"You've got it, Sergeant!" Len and Malcolm started cackling again.

Shadow's head was beginning to hurt listening to the double act, and he couldn't see the point in staying any longer. He thanked Len and Malcolm for their help and motioned for Jimmy to follow him.

Chapter Three

Down 2 (6 letters)
No sip, Olive! It could kill you

They stepped out of Len's dressing room and found Angela, who had changed out of her costume and seemed to have regained her composure, waiting for them. Standing next to her, still looking agitated, was Rohan: the tall, bespectacled young man who had been playing the evil henchman.

"I'm sorry, I know you wanted to talk to us all, Chief Inspector," began Angela, "but one of the little girls' parents' aren't here. They were having dinner over in Harrogate and thought she'd be having a sleepover with her friend who is one of the other dwarves, but she's upset about what happened and wants to go home instead. I said I'd take her to meet her mum and dad. Rohan has offered to drive us. Is that okay with you, Chief Inspector?"

"Yes, of course, Angela," agreed Shadow, "but if it does turn out Spencer didn't die of natural causes, we might still need to speak to all the children."

Angela grimaced but nodded. "They are all in my class at

school, but let's hope it doesn't come to that," she said, turning away.

"One more thing, Angela," Shadow called after her. She stopped and turned back. "Who gave you the bottle of green liquid before you came onstage?"

"Nobody gave it to me. It was waiting for me on the prop table. Everything is laid out there in the order it's going to be used onstage." She pointed to a long wooden trellis table waiting in the wings, then she and Rohan disappeared back into her dressing room.

The two detectives approached the table that was covered in all sorts of paraphernalia. There were some carrots for the pantomime horse, another handbag for the dame, the picks and axes for the dwarves and a basket of apples for Snow White.

"That's a point," said Jimmy. "I thought it was meant to be Snow White who was poisoned, not Prince Charming."

"I don't think accuracy was this production's top priority," replied Shadow, "but get forensics to check those apples for poison anyway." His eyes quickly scanned other the items then stopped when he spotted something he recognised.

"But at least we know where the major's missing antique sabre is now," he said, pointing to a gleaming sword with a curved blade.

"Really? Is that it? Are you sure, Chief?" asked Jimmy.

"Yes, look at the crest on the handle."

Jimmy took his phone out of his pocket and tapped at

the screen a few times. He squinted at the photos he'd been sent, then down at the ornate weapon on the table.

"You're right, Chief. What's it doing here?"

"Waiting to be used in a fight scene by the look of it," replied Shadow, who had an uncomfortable feeling that Spencer Knight's death was looking less and less like it was due to natural causes.

"I think there was meant to be a sword fight between Prince Charming and the queen's henchman. Angela was telling me Rohan was quite nervous about it."

"I'm not surprised if they were using real swords."

"Look, Chief, the other sword is clearly fake. You can tell as soon as you pick it up. It's made of wood with a metal coating, so it makes a clashing sound. Why would someone put a real sword here?"

"To make a point!" quipped Ben, who had appeared from the stage.

"I won't tell you again," growled Shadow as the chuckling scientist waved an evidence bag containing a bottle of green liquid in front of his face. "What have you got there? I thought the bottle was empty."

"This is a different bottle, Chief. A full one. Ollie, Sophie and I were chatting. We thought if the bottle Sophie had did turn out to have poison in it, then it would have been quicker and easier for the killer to replace the bottle itself rather than empty the contents and refill it. That's a bit of a faff. If that was the case, then they would need to have hidden the original bottle somewhere, so Ollie and I started poking about and I found this buried in the sand." He pointed to the red fire bucket on the floor next to the prop table. Shadow felt as if a heavy weight had just settled on his shoulders. It looked like they could definitely forget about natural causes.

"Wow! Good work, Ben!" exclaimed Jimmy.

"Yes, well done," conceded Shadow. "Right, gentlemen, now we know we probably are dealing with a murder, let's find out who is responsible for the props."

"I can help you there, Chief Inspector," said Len Horning, who had appeared without any of them noticing. "It's the marvellous Miss Edmundson. Susan Edmundson."

"I know her," said Jimmy. "She used to work in the office at Angela's school, but she retired."

"She's been part of our merry band for years. She's in charge of props and costumes. She's quite the seamstress. I call her our wardrobe mistress, but she doesn't like it. Says it has 'connotations'."

"And where might I find Miss Edmundson?" asked Shadow, his patience starting to wear thin again.

"Malcolm sent her home. She was in quite a state about what happened to Spencer."

"Did nobody hear me when I asked for everyone involved in the production to remain here?" replied Shadow, trying not to sound exasperated.

"Oh, Susan wouldn't have been any use to you. She

looked like she was going to keel over any moment, poor thing. You wouldn't want another casualty on your hands now, would you, Chief Inspector?"

"Thank you, Mr Horning. You are free to go too," said Shadow firmly. "And if I could ask you not to mention the incident this evening to anyone until the circumstances of Mr Knight's death have been established. I understand you have a radio programme, but—"

"I'm shocked you could think such a thing, Chief Inspector," interrupted Len dramatically. "I'll have you know I'm the soul of discretion. Not that it matters much. Half the city saw what happened onstage tonight." And with that he strutted back down the corridor.

"Should I call Major Armitage and tell him we've found his sabre?" asked Jimmy when the pantomime dame had disappeared.

"No," replied Shadow thoughtfully. "At least not yet. He was here earlier. Did you see him?"

Jimmy shook his head. "No. Who was he with?"

"Nobody. He was here alone, and he disappeared in the interval." He turned to Ben, who was still looking proud of himself. "Can you take the sabre back to the lab with you and check for fingerprints, traces of blood and anything else unusual you can think of?"

"No problem, Chief. I'll see if we've got a bag big enough. Oh, and by the way, Sophie wanted to know if it's okay to move the body now?"

Shadow nodded. "Yes, that's fine," he agreed. The scientist disappeared, and a few seconds later Shadow and Jimmy stepped to one side and lowered their heads as the body on the stretcher was quietly carried past them. They weren't the only ones to see Spencer being carried away. From the far end of the corridor came the sound of loud sobbing. Shadow turned and saw Lottie, still in her Snow White costume, dash back into her dressing room, tears streaming down her face.

"Should we speak to her now or wait until she calms down, Chief?" asked Jimmy.

"Let's go now, before she disappears like our prop lady and pantomime horse," he replied. Shadow was about to knock on Snow White's dressing room door when it was opened and the older man, dressed in black, who had been comforting her earlier stepped out.

"I'm sorry, Chief Inspector. I know you wanted to speak to us all, but I really don't think my Lottie is up to it. She's very sensitive at the best of times. Can I take her home and I promise we'll come and see you in the morning?"

"Can I ask your name?" asked Shadow.

"Stanley Beresford, sir. I'm Lottie's dad."

Before Shadow could respond, Jimmy had thrust his hand out.

"I'm Sergeant Chang, Mr Beresford. We spoke earlier today about the missing sabre."

A flicker of confusion crossed Stanley Beresford's face as he shook Jimmy's hand, but before he could say anything,

Shadow stepped in.

"If Sergeant Chang already has your details, then perhaps we could visit you both tomorrow instead, Mr Beresford. Your daughter may feel more comfortable talking at home."

"Yes, that would be better, thank you, Chief Inspector," replied Stanley.

"Then we'll wish you a good evening and I hope Lottie feels better soon."

Stanley merely nodded then stepped back into the dressing room without another word. The two detectives walked back down the corridor.

"I wasn't going to say anything about finding the sabre, you know," whispered Jimmy.

"I'm glad to hear it. I think it's best we don't say anything about finding it to anyone until we hear back from Ben and Ollie," Shadow hissed back. They were now in the wings. On the stage, police tape had cordoned off the area where Spencer had fallen. Ben and Ollie were still working and chuckling to themselves. Shadow turned to Jimmy. "We may as well go home. I don't think there is anyone left for us to speak to. We'll start again in the morning when, hopefully, Sophie will be able to tell us exactly what killed Spencer Knight. Before you go, check with Malcolm Webster that you have everyone's contact details, then send him on his way too."

Shadow walked through the eerily empty auditorium and out through the foyer, nodding to several uniformed officers who were still on duty.

"Chief! The press are still hanging about," called out Tom, who was coming down the stairs behind him. "I thought I should warn you."

"MacNab?"

"Yes. Malcolm had invited him to review tonight's performance."

Shadow grunted then noticed the constable's arms were full of camera equipment.

"Jimmy said you were filming the performance."

"That's right, Chief."

"Good. Let me have a copy of the recording as soon as you can. I'll see you tomorrow."

The Minster bells were striking midnight when he stepped out into the cold night air. As Tom had warned, MacNab and a photographer were waiting by the entrance. They both sprang forward when they spotted Shadow.

"Chief Inspector Shadow, can you confirm that a man died here tonight? Is it true you and two of your colleagues witnessed his death? Can you confirm the dead man is Spencer Knight? Are you treating his death as suspicious?"

Shadow ignored the barrage of questions and merely snapped "No comment" in response as he put his head down and continued on his way. Fortunately, the rain had stopped, but the temperature had dropped under the clear sky and his breath formed little clouds in front of him as he walked. He was deep in thought and halfway down Parliament Street when he stopped abruptly, remembering his suitcase was still in his office. Cursing to himself, he turned and headed back to the station.

Twenty minutes later, he was trudging along the towpath, lugging his case along and dodging puddles where the swollen river had spilled over on to the bank. He was sure his case hadn't felt this heavy when he'd left Italy forty-eight hours ago. The three geese that were huddled together on *Florence*'s roof watched him approach silently with their beady black eyes.

"Perhaps you'll appreciate me after living with a dog for a few weeks," he muttered as he stepped aboard, hauling his case after him. He unlocked the door and flicked on the light. The place was spotless. Far cleaner and tidier than when he'd left it. He'd been braced for the smell of wet dog but there was no trace of the previous occupants except for a handle on one of the cupboards in the galley kitchen. For months it had been hanging off, but now it was once again screwed firmly to the door. He went through to his bedroom and found the bed had been made with fresh sheets and all corners neatly tucked under, betraying Jake's previous life in the army. The bathroom was equally immaculate. He removed his jacket and tie and returned to the sitting room.

He opened his suitcase and rummaged through the dirty laundry until he found one of the bottles of wine from Luca's vineyard. Bianca, Luca's wife, had insisted on packing him up a couple of them, along with a box of her handmade almond biscuits. His hosts were equally insistent about sending several cases of their next vintage to him. He opened the bottle and poured himself a large glass. As he took the first sip, he was immediately transported from cold, damp North Yorkshire, back to the Grecos' sun-drenched family home in the countryside near Lecce.

While he was there, they had spent most evenings sitting on the terrace overlooking the vines, eating and listening to Luca tell stories, mainly about Luisa. It had been over thirty since she'd died, and he barely ever spoke about her. It had felt good to be with people who remembered her as clearly as he did and had loved her as much as he had. He'd visited places she'd told him about and Luca had taken him to see her grave. He'd stood in the shade of the olive trees, tracing her name on the gravestone with his fingers and wishing he hadn't waited so long to pay his respects.

After supper, Luca and Bianca's four children had often joined them too, sometimes arguing, sometimes joking but never silent. In comparison, *Florence* felt very quiet, yet while he'd been away, he'd missed being here. Despite what Jimmy might have thought, he'd never had any intention of not returning. If Luisa had lived, perhaps the two of them could have made a life together in her home country. Now, it was too late. His life was here. His work and the people he knew and who knew him. Then as the Italian sun had tanned his face, he'd found himself worrying if Sophie or Rose were upset about how the wedding had ended and wondering what Maggie was doing.

He looked down at the shirts and socks spilling out of the case on to the floor. He'd been planning on taking them to the laundry and asking Maggie out to dinner, but now she was going away to Spain. Not that there was any guarantee she would have accepted anyway. She had definitely been a little cool when they'd bumped into her earlier, but he couldn't work out why. While he was having supper at the Golden Dragon, Rose had rather pointedly asked if he'd contacted Maggie while he was away.

"To wish her a happy Christmas or let her know when you planned to return," she'd said, fixing her dark, intelligent eyes on him.

"No, I didn't want to bother her. Besides, it seems some people didn't think I would return," he'd murmured, frowning at Jimmy, but Rose had merely clicked her tongue as she'd cleared away the plates.

He told himself it was true. He hadn't liked to bother Maggie, especially over the festive period when she was sure to be busy with her enormous extended family. Now he thought perhaps he should have done. After all, it was Maggie who had bought him the plane ticket and persuaded him to go to Italy in the first place. What had she said? That it was time he said goodbye? He'd done just that when he'd laid a bouquet of white roses on Luisa's grave. He didn't know how long he'd sat there under the olive tree thinking about her and their life together and what could have been.

Now, thanks to Luca and Bianca, he could remember the good times they had shared without being stabbed by the pain of regret. But just because he'd laid his past to rest didn't mean his future was looking any clearer. He downed the last of his wine. He couldn't think about any of that now. He needed to go to sleep. Tomorrow, he had a murder to investigate.

THE NEXT MORNING, despite his late night, he was awake early and arrived at Bettys as they were opening. The only thing to spoil his breakfast was his neighbour's reading material. As the smartly dressed grey-haired lady held up her copy of the *York Herald*, he noticed the headline on the front page.

> Panto Death – police enjoy show as Prince Charming collapses

It didn't help that the article was accompanied by a photo of a grinning Spencer Knight and another of Jimmy, Ben and Ollie all in their neck braces trooping out of the theatre and looking every bit as cheerful as the dead man.

"For crying out loud! You would think they'd have the brains not to leave together," he muttered as he stood up and went to pay his bill.

He arrived at the station to find Jimmy in the process of

setting up an incident room. A whiteboard was now covered with photographs. Spencer Knight's was in the middle and surrounded by images of most of his fellow cast members. Not for the first time, Shadow was struck by his sergeant's similarity to an excitable Labrador puppy as Jimmy came bounding over to him.

"Morning, Chief. Guess what?" he asked eagerly.

"Sophie has confirmed Spencer Knight was poisoned."

"Yes. It was an overdose of methadone. Sophie is still waiting for the blood test results to see exactly how much was in his system, but it was found in liquid form in the bottle Spencer drank from. Sophie said it would be odourless and although it might have tasted bitter, it probably wouldn't have been noticeable mixed with the lime cordial and green food colouring that were in the bottle too. The bottle Ben found only contained the cordial and colouring."

"Then let's start looking for suspects," said Shadow, turning his attention to the board covered in photos. Surrounding Spencer were Malcolm, Len Horning, Lottie Beresford, Stan Beresford, Steve and Matt West, Rohan and an older woman Jimmy had labelled as Susan Edmundson.

"Those are all the people who had access to backstage," explained Jimmy. "Um, I haven't put Tom up there obviously or Angela because, well, I know she was the last person to handle the bottle Knight drank from…" he paused "…but she is my sister. Is that okay, Chief?"

"Yes, Sergeant Chang, it is okay. If Angela turns out to

be our killer, I will retire on the spot. Get a photo of our missing evil queen too – Francesca, wasn't it?"

"Yes, Chief. Francesca French," replied Jimmy as he started tapping away at his keyboard.

"Let's add Major Armitage as well. I want to know why he left the theatre early. I don't suppose Ben and Ollie have been in touch about the sabre yet?"

Jimmy paused briefly to check his phone. "No, not yet."

"See if you can get a plan of the theatre as well, particularly the backstage area."

"I have one here, Chief," said Tom, who had just walked through the door carrying a sheet of paper. "I printed it off while I was waiting for the recording of last night's performance to download. I've emailed it to you, Jimmy." He unfolded the plan and laid it out on the desk in front of them. "I've marked up who was in which dressing room. There is only one entrance to the backstage area down this corridor that leads from the bar area. There's a fire escape here, but that's bolted from the inside, and the only other way of accessing the backstage area is from the stage itself."

"Could someone have unbolted the fire door in advance and then sneaked in via the fire escape?" suggested Jimmy.

Tom shook his head. "I don't think so. It would have been pretty risky. Someone would have been bound to spot a stranger."

Shadow half listened to his colleagues as he studied the plan for a moment, then looked up at the photos.

"If we do include Major Armitage and Francesca French, we could be looking at ten possible suspects. And if Malcolm and Len are to be believed, Spencer could quite possibly have made enemies of any of them both in his professional and personal life. Let's work on trying to eliminate a few or at least try to prioritise them. What about Malcolm Webster? I really don't want to have to endure questioning him again if we don't need to."

"We both saw him sitting on the front row during the performance," said Jimmy.

"What about during the interval? Did he go backstage then?"

"No, Chief," supplied Tom. "Malcolm was in the bar for the entire interval. Most of the time he was bending the ear of MacNab. It sounded like he was trying to make sure they were going to get a glowing review. He even bought Kevin a drink and Malcolm never usually puts his hand in his pocket for anyone."

Shadow nodded thoughtfully. "If Malcolm was so keen for a decent review, surely he wouldn't jeopardise the production by killing the leading man."

"We can probably rule out Rohan too. He's only been in York for a few months and barely knows anyone. Angela brought him to Mum's for a meal a couple of times and he seems like a nice kid. Right, Tom?"

Tom nodded his head in agreement.

"All right, we'll just leave him as a witness for now.

Thanks, Tom. Can you get to work on trying to find Knight's next of kin?"

The constable disappeared, and Shadow turned back to Jimmy.

"That still leaves us with a lot of possible suspects. We need to speak to Miss Edmundson and find out exactly when she placed the bottle of poison out on the prop table. Then Lottie and Stanley Beresford. I want to see if what Angela and Tom said is true and Lottie really was in a relationship with the victim."

"It would explain why she was so upset."

"Yes, but it could lead to a possible motive too," mused Shadow. "Is there anyone else we are waiting to speak to?"

"I've left messages for Francesca French to contact me, but so far nothing," replied Jimmy. "By the way, before I left the theatre last night, I spoke to Diane and Derek Dawson – you know the sound and lighting team Malcolm told us about. They are old friends of his and live on the Isle of Wight. They are only up in York for a few weeks because their daughter works at one of the insurance companies here and is expecting their first grandchild. She's already nearly two weeks overdue. The doctors are talking about inducing her on Monday."

Shadow held up his hand.

"Is any of this relevant to Spencer Knight's death?"

"No, not really, except to explain they were only here by chance. They only met Knight once briefly at a read-through, and they said he spent a while chatting to them about their pension provision. Tom was upstairs filming right next to them. He said he would have noticed if either of them came into the bar, but they didn't so I think we can rule them out, Chief."

"That's something, I suppose. Right, let's start with Susan Edmundson. Have we got an address for her?"

"I've got her home address. I tried phoning her landline just before you arrived but there was no answer. However, Tom mentioned that she works for Knight and French Associates."

"I thought you said she was retired."

"From working at Angela's school. She was the bursar's assistant there. She left about a year ago, but according to Angela, she got bored and started working part-time for Spencer Knight as a sort of bookkeeper/receptionist/secretary. When I checked again, I realised the address for Knight and French Associates is the same as Spencer's home address. He must have worked from home."

"Then let's go there first. We might come across Susan Edmundson, and if we're lucky, we might even find the elusive Ms French too," said Shadow. The two of them headed out of the door and down the stairs.

"Do you think we'll be long, Chief?" asked Jimmy.

Shadow raised an eyebrow. "Do you have something more pressing than a murder to investigate, Sergeant?"

"I said I'd go round to the school this afternoon. Angela

is going to sit with the children while I ask them a few questions," explained Jimmy as the two of them left the station and walked down Coney Street. He handed Shadow a list of the seven children's names and ages. Four boys and three girls, and they were all either ten or eleven years old. "I thought they would be more relaxed talking to me in their classroom instead of asking them to come to the station. I thought it might be less intimidating if I went alone too, unless you want to come with me, of course."

"No, no you go ahead," Shadow replied quickly, handing the list back. He could think of nothing he would enjoy less than spending an hour trying to get sense out of seven excitable schoolchildren. They paused at the end of Spurriergate for the traffic to come to a halt, and Jimmy lowered his voice.

"You don't think one of the kids could be the killer, do you? I watched this TV series about children who kill. It was really disturbing."

"I think it is highly unlikely, and I've told you before about basing your theories on television programmes. But look on the bright side, if one of them does turn out to be a murderer, they are all over the age of criminal responsibility, so at least you can charge them."

As they crossed Skeldergate Bridge and made their way towards Bishopthorpe Road, Jimmy busied himself making and taking phone calls. First Tom called to say it appeared that Spencer Knight had no next of kin. Then he telephoned the Beresfords and arranged to see them later that morning.

"They live over in South Bank, so we should have plenty of time to walk over there when we've finished at Knight's place."

"Good," replied Shadow, who avoided driving as much as possible. They turned on to what the locals called Bishy Road. Despite being close to Skeldergate Bridge, it wasn't an area of the city he knew well. As they walked along, he took in the range of delis, antiques shops and galleries and the cafés full of glossy-haired young mothers, sipping frothy coffees and herbal teas. Jimmy was right, the area would be perfect for him and Sophie. He could easily imagine them in one of the smart terraced houses. Not that he voiced this thought to his sergeant. A brief glance in an estate agent's window they passed by told him that the area was expensive even for York.

However, it turned out that Spencer Knight did not live in a house but in the penthouse of a large apartment block. The art deco building had once been one of the many chocolate factories that the city was so famous for. Jimmy used the keys they had found in Spencer's pocket to let them into the building. They walked through the plush reception area and took the lift up to the top floor. Jimmy was about to let them into the penthouse too, but Shadow stopped him. There was a faint humming sound coming from the behind the door.

"Is someone hoovering?" whispered Jimmy.

"Let's find out," replied Shadow, knocking briskly on the door. The humming sound stopped and a second later, the door was opened by woman wearing a navy suit and court shoes. Her face was make-up-free except for a dash of pink lipstick, and her grey chin-length hair was held back from her face by two tortoiseshell combs. The skin beneath her eyes was slightly damp, and in her hand, she was clutching a white cotton handkerchief.

"Yes, how may I help you?" she asked.

Shadow showed her his warrant card. "My name is Chief Inspector Shadow and this is Sergeant Chang. We're investigating the death of Spencer Knight. Would you be Miss Susan Edmundson?"

"That's correct," replied the woman, but said no more.

"May we come in?" he asked.

She paused as if thinking of a way she could refuse, before finally replying, "Very well, but I must ask you to remove your shoes first."

Shadow glanced at Jimmy, who looked bemused.

"Mr Knight's carpets were only shampooed last week. They show the dirt very easily," Miss Edmundson insisted.

Shadow reluctantly slipped off both his shoes and Jimmy did the same with his trainers as Susan Edmundson quickly disappeared back into the apartment.

"I hope nobody nicks them. They're brand new," complained Jimmy.

"I'm sure they'll be fine. Besides, how many people wear

size fourteens? Why aren't you wearing any socks?" asked Shadow, looking down at his sergeant's bare feet.

"I didn't have any clean ones. I was going to call in at Mum's and pick some up from there, but I overslept."

"You're a grown man. Why is your mother still doing your washing?"

"She's not, but Soph and I have been really busy, and I've still got a few things in my old bedroom. Wow, look at this place."

The two of them stopped bickering and took in their surroundings. The apartment was a vast open-plan design and minimalistic. One wall was a floor-to-ceiling window that gave spectacular views across the racecourse. Three pale grey leather sofas were arranged in a U-shape around a huge flat-screen television mounted on the wall at the far end of the room. A glass-topped eight-seater dining table stood in the middle of the room and on top of that was a marble sculpture of a naked woman. A few black and white photos of racing cars adorned the walls, and the carpet Miss Edmundson was so keen to protect was pure white. Shadow's first thought was that there were clearly no children or dogs in Spencer Knight's life.

The buzzing noise they had heard outside the door began again. In the corner behind them was a large white desk with two smaller desks on either side. Miss Edmundson was sitting at one of the desks and feeding sheet after sheet of paper into the shredder at her feet. The bin beneath the shredder was almost overflowing. The two detectives hurried over.

"May I ask what you are shredding, Miss Edmundson?" asked Shadow.

"Just some confidential papers. Spencer took his clients' security very seriously."

She started feeding another sheet into the machine, but Shadow reached out and put his hand on her arm.

"I'd like you to stop, please. It's possible you could be destroying evidence."

"What do you mean evidence?"

"We don't believe Mr Knight died of natural causes."

Susan Edmundson stared back at him. At first, she'd looked like she wanted to argue with him. Now she looked confused.

"Who on earth would do such a thing? Spencer was a wonderful man."

"Have you been working for him long?"

"About eight months. I work part-time. Mornings only."

"And Mr Knight worked from home?"

"He did. Although the nature of his work meant he was often out visiting clients."

"Ms French, his business partner. Did she work here too?"

Miss Edmundson's face hardened. "Oh, she's sometimes here."

"Have you seen or heard from Ms French? Is she aware

of Mr Knight's death?"

"I've no idea where she is or what she is or isn't aware of."

"Did Mr Knight's clients visit him here?"

"He preferred to call on clients at their own homes or offices. Occasionally, clients might come here, but that was usually outside of normal working hours."

"Do you know if he'd had a disagreement with any of his clients recently?"

"What people don't realise is that he's not a magician, Chief Inspector. There is always a little risk involved in any investment. They see how well Spencer has done for himself but don't realise how hard he works."

Shadow noted she hadn't actually answered his question.

"Do you know if he had arranged to meet any clients yesterday?"

"No, but I didn't keep his diary. All his appointments were scheduled on his laptop and synched with his phone." Shadow looked around the office area. There were three desktop computers but so sign of any laptop.

"We have his phone but not his laptop. Do you know where it might be?"

"No, he'd misplaced it over the weekend. He thought he might have left it at the golf club."

Shadow wasn't quite sure he believed her. He started to cough loudly. "Could I trouble you for a glass of water, please?" he asked.

Again, Miss Edmundson looked like she wanted to refuse but instead nodded reluctantly and headed towards a door on the other side of the room that Shadow assumed led to the kitchen. When she was out of sight, he turned to Jimmy.

"Get the finance team to come over here," he instructed quietly. "I want them to go through these computers and find out if Knight was up to anything dodgy." While Jimmy made the phone call, Shadow quickly opened each of the desk drawers. There was no sign of the missing laptop, but he did find two sets of car keys. Jimmy finished his call and gave a low whistle when he saw them.

"Looks like his wheels matched his home, Chief."

At that moment, Susan Edmundson hurried back into the room, carrying a single cut-glass tumbler of water and eyeing the two of them suspiciously.

Shadow thanked her and took a sip from the glass. "We had hoped to speak to you last night at the theatre."

"Malcolm said I could go home. I was very upset. Spencer and I were very close."

Shadow exchanged a look with Jimmy. Malcolm and Len had implied Spencer was a womaniser but could that include Susan Edmundson? Shadow thought it unlikely but decided to bite the bullet.

"Was your relationship purely professional, Miss Edmundson?"

She turned slightly pink and began to blink rapidly. "Completely. Spencer was an absolute gentleman. He would never abuse his position as my employer in that way. We trusted each other implicitly."

Shadow nodded and quickly moved on. "We understand you were in charge of the prop table backstage at the theatre."

"That's correct."

"Do you remember placing the green bottle of liquid that Mr Knight drank from on the table?"

"Yes, I do. It was about ten minutes before the interval during the last song of act three. All the props for the first half had been taken so the table was empty. The bottle was the last prop I put out. I poured the lime cordial and green colouring in very precisely. I didn't want it to make it too bitter. I hope you aren't suggesting I poisoned Spencer, Chief Inspector."

"I simply want to know how long the bottle was on display for and who could have interfered with it."

"Well, anybody could. During the interval everyone was dashing back and forth. Ideally, I would have been by the table keeping an eye on things, but it was very hectic. Francesca had let us down, so Angela had to go on in her place, which meant I was left in charge of the children when she was onstage. Rohan helped out too, but quite frankly the little monsters were rather a handful."

"Did any of the cast or crew leave the backstage area during the interval?"

"No, I don't think so. Malcolm was very particular about

preserving the mystique of the performance."

"Did you see anyone come backstage? Friends or relatives perhaps?"

"No, but as I said, I was run off my feet, making sure all the dwarves had been to the loo. If it was up to me, they wouldn't have been allowed to eat or drink anything until after the performance, like the West boys."

"Do you recall putting two swords, one with a curved blade, out on the table too?"

"Yes, for the fight between Spencer and Rohan. The swords were first then the dwarves' axes had to be lined up next to them. The dwarves were meant to join in the fight too, you see," she explained.

"You didn't notice anything strange about one of the swords at all?" asked Jimmy.

"No, why?"

Shadow shot Jimmy a warning look. He still didn't want anyone to know about the sabre yet.

"Thank you. You have been very helpful, Miss Edmundson, but we won't keep you any longer."

"But I must stay here. What happens if any of Spencer's clients call?"

"Some of our officers will be arriving shortly. I am sure they will be able to deal with any enquiries. May I also ask you to leave the keys you have to this apartment?"

She looked mutinous again, but picked up her large navy handbag and produced a set of keys neatly labelled "Mr

Knight's Office" which she handed to Shadow.

"Thank you," he said. "Before you go, Miss Edmundson… There are two sets of car keys here. Did Mr Knight own two cars?" asked Shadow.

"He certainly did. The Porsche and the Range Rover are both parked outside. The penthouse comes with two parking spaces."

Jimmy went over to the window and looked down on to the car park and confirmed to Shadow with a nod that both vehicles were there.

"He always ordered a taxi to take him to the theatre," explained Miss Edmundson, "so he could enjoy a drink afterwards."

"Didn't Ms French use one of the spaces?" asked Shadow.

Susan Edmundson bridled a little. "No, she did not, Chief Inspector. Ms French was allowed to use the visitors' car park."

"Ms French missed the performance last night. Do you know why?"

"I have no idea, Chief Inspector. I always found her to be a selfish and unreliable woman. I am surprised Mr Knight put up with her." And with that she turned on her heel and stalked out of the apartment.

Chapter Four

Down 6 (5 letters)
Bears' claws may be as sharp as this sword

After the door had slammed shut behind Susan Edmundson, Shadow knelt down and inspected the contents of the shredder bin.

"What are the chances of piecing any of this together, do you think?"

Jimmy picked up a few strands of paper and squinted at them.

"I've heard the FBI can do it."

"I somehow doubt they'll be interested in helping us but get it all bagged up and see if Ben and Ollie can do anything with it. Let's look at the rest of the place while we wait for finance to turn up."

Unlike the rest of the apartment, Spencer's bedroom was decorated in the style of a gentleman's club. Everything was dark wood and leather with tartan curtains and bedding. Jimmy gave a deep sigh as they entered.

"What's wrong?" asked Shadow.

"Me and Sophie would never be able to afford this place,

even if it does come on the market."

"Never mind," replied Shadow, who personally thought the place was rather soulless despite the magnificent view of the racecourse.

"I always wanted one of those too," said Jimmy, pointing to the drinks globe standing next to the small brown chesterfield sofa in the corner.

"What on earth for? You barely drink."

"I know but it's kind of retro. Makes me think of James Bond."

Shadow wasn't listening. His attention had been drawn to the framed photographs that covered the chest of drawers and dressing table. They were all of Spencer with a series of different women. Several were of the woman he recognised from the programme as Francesca French. She and Spencer were in various exotic beach locations; however, the two photos on the bedside table were of Spencer with a much younger, prettier blonde girl. In each of them, they seemed to be in what looked like expensive restaurants or wine bars. He picked up one of the pictures for a closer look.

"Is that Lottie Beresford?" he asked.

Jimmy came over and nodded. "Yep, that's her. She's a natural blonde. She wore a dark wig to play Snow White."

"It certainly looks like the two of them were more than just fellow thespians, and it seems Malcolm and Len were right about Spencer Knight being quite the ladies' man. Let's get all these photos bagged up too and get someone to come and collect them."

While Jimmy made yet another phone call, Shadow moved through into the en-suite bathroom but except for a vast collection of expensive aftershaves, found nothing else of note.

Next was the kitchen. It was modern, minimalistic and looked like it had barely been used. The fridge contained little except some milk, a dish of strawberries and half a dozen bottles of champagne. As Shadow inspected the victim's wine collection, there was a knock at the door. Jimmy – his phone still to his ear – went to answer it. It was the finance team, who consisted of two young women. Always dressed in black trouser suits, confusingly, they were both called Jane. They were thorough and extremely diligent. They also spoke very quickly and used a startling number of abbreviations and acronyms. Shadow always found it easier to let his sergeant liaise with them and merely nodded politely in their direction as he scooped up the two sets of car keys before leaving the apartment.

Down in the car park, he searched through the Porsche and the Range Rover, but there was no sign of the missing laptop in either. However, there were several long blonde hairs on the passenger seat of the Porsche. After seeing the photos of Spencer and Lottie together, Shadow was fairly sure they belonged to her, unless there was yet another woman in Spencer Knight's life.

"Any chance we could take this for a spin to the Beresfords', Chief?" asked Jimmy when he caught up with him.

"None at all. Besides with that thing on your neck you'll never get behind the wheel and it was you who said they were in walking distance. Now get those hairs in one of your evidence bags and ask Ben and Ollie to find out who they belong to."

Then he locked both cars and gave the keys to Jimmy to put in one of his many evidence bags, then they set off back down Bishy Road in the direction of South Bank.

"What do we know about Stanley and Lottie Beresford?" asked Shadow.

Jimmy began reading from his electronic notebook as they walked along. "Stanley Beresford is forty-five years old. He joined the army straight out of school and saw active service in Iraq and Afghanistan. He rose to the rank of sergeant major. Since leaving the army three years ago, he's worked part-time for a local building firm. He left the army so he could look after Ann, his wife who had been diagnosed with cancer. She died about a year ago. They'd been married for twenty years and Charlotte, or Lottie, is their only child. She's eighteen, will be doing her A levels in the summer and has already accepted a place at drama school down in London. She starts there in September. Neither have any criminal convictions. This is their house."

They stopped outside a small red-brick house in the middle of one of the terraces that had been built to accommodate the workers in the nearby chocolate factory. Jimmy knocked on the door and after a few seconds it was opened by Stanley. He was dressed in jeans and a Help for Heroes hoodie and looked younger but no happier than when they had seen him the night before. He was tall and muscular, and his facial features looked like they had been chiselled out of stone. His dark hair was cut very short and was peppered with grey.

"You'd better come in," he said by way of a greeting. The two detectives followed him down the narrow hallway and through into the kitchen at the back of the house. It was tidy and scrupulously clean. The white units and worktops were spotless, the chrome taps and draining board gleamed, and there was a faint smell of disinfectant. A small table with three chairs was in the centre of the room and an archway led into a cosy sitting area. Stanley directed them to sit down on the armchairs that were placed either side of the fireplace. The walls were covered in family photos including several of Stanley in his dress uniform, but most were of Lottie at various ages starting from when she was a baby. Sitting in a basket by the electric fire was a whippet wearing a cone around his neck and looking very sorry for himself.

"Who's this?" asked Jimmy, who was already on his knees making a fuss of the dog.

"That's Arthur."

"Arthur the regimental whippet?"

"That's right. He lives with us. No wonder he likes you. With that thing on your neck, the two of you match," observed Stanley wryly as Arthur began licking Jimmy's hand. "Do you want a cup of tea? I've just made myself one."

"No thank you, Mr Beresford," replied Shadow, and Jimmy stiffly shook his head as he reluctantly left Arthur and opened his electronic notebook.

"So have you found out how Knight died yet?" asked Stanley as he carried his mug of tea from the kitchen and settled into the sofa opposite the two detectives.

"He was poisoned," replied Shadow.

Stanley didn't comment. He simply nodded and took a drink of his tea.

"You don't seem surprised," said Shadow.

"I'm not. A man like Spencer Knight makes plenty of enemies. Seems a strange way to get rid of him though. In front of everyone like that."

"Did you know him well?"

"Well enough."

"Your daughter seemed very upset by his death."

"Of course she was. She's a sensitive young girl, and it isn't long since she lost her mum."

Stanley nodded towards a framed photo on the middle of the ledge above the fire. It showed a younger Lottie in her school uniform with her parents proudly beaming on either side. Ann Beresford had been an attractive woman with the same bright blue eyes and blonde hair as her daughter.

"Was Lottie in a relationship with Spencer?"

Stanley's eyes flashed angrily but his tone remained the

same.

"It wasn't a relationship. He'd turned her head, that's all. Flattering her and taking her to posh restaurants. A man his age should have known better and left her alone."

"Did you ask him to?"

"He knew how I felt, but he wouldn't back off."

"That must have made you angry," suggested Shadow.

Stanley placed his mug down on the table, leant forward and looked him straight in the eye. "Everything about that man made me angry, but if you're asking did I kill him? Then the answer is no. Am I pleased he's gone? Yes. Not that I like to see Lottie upset, but he was no good. She and the rest of the world are better off without him."

Shadow nodded. "Can I ask you about the sabre that went missing after the regimental dinner?"

Stanley looked surprised by the change of direction. "What's that got to do with anything?"

"We found it. It was on the prop table last night."

"How did it get there?"

"I was hoping you could tell us. It was about to be used in a fight scene between Spencer Knight and Rohan Kapoor."

"We thought it had been taken as a joke by one of the lads."

"It was you who discovered it was missing?" confirmed Shadow.

"Yes, but…"

"And you were there on the night of the regimental dinner?"

"I dropped off Arthur, but I didn't stay. It was serving officers only."

"Did you return to collect Arthur?"

"Yes. Rohan gave me a lift. He wanted to check on Arthur too."

"What's Rohan's connection to Arthur?" asked Shadow, glancing over to the whippet, who kept emitting the occasional sorrowful whine.

"He's been working with Owen Treadwell, the vet. Owen operated on Arthur when he broke his leg chasing a squirrel. Daft bugger! You're not as young as you used to be, are you, lad!" Arthur whimpered again and turned his cone-encased head away as if deeply hurt by the comment. "The wound got infected so Rohan has been keeping an eye on it."

"Is that why he's wearing the collar?" asked Jimmy.

"Yes. He hates it, but it should only be for a couple more days now."

Jimmy smiled sympathetically. "And is that why he's living with you and not at the regimental headquarters?"

"No, he's lived with us for a while. Lottie loves dogs, and Major Armitage thought he might cheer her up when her mum got ill."

"That was kind of him," commented Shadow.

Stanley nodded and gave a small smile. "He's a good man, the major."

"He was at the theatre last night. Did you see him?"

"No," replied Stanley quickly.

"I thought he might have been there to wish Lottie good luck."

"I never saw him," repeated Stanley.

"Perhaps Lottie did. Could we to speak to her, please?"

Stanley looked like he wanted to refuse, but instead said, "If you must. But try not to upset her."

He stood up and left the kitchen. Shadow could hear him calling up the stairs for his daughter before returning.

Shadow cleared his throat. "It might be better if we talk to Lottie alone."

Stanley looked wary. "Why?"

"In my experience, teenagers speak more freely when their parents aren't around, and she is over eighteen."

"I suppose you are right, but try not to upset her," he repeated. At that moment Lottie appeared. She too was dressed in jeans and a hoodie and looked younger. Her pretty face was make-up-free, and her long blonde hair was tied in a loose ponytail.

"It's the police from last night, love. I said they'd be coming," her father explained. "They want to have a word with you about, well, last night. I'll stay if you want me to."

Lottie shook her head. "It's okay. I'll be fine, Dad."

Stan looked disappointed but nodded. "Right then, I'll be out in the shed if you need me."

Reluctantly, he left through the back door, and Shadow

watched him walk to the shed at the end of the long, thin garden. He kept glancing back over his shoulder as he went. Lottie took his place on the sofa, one leg curled beneath her. Arthur immediately trotted over, and she gently lifted him on to her knee. Despite her father's warnings, Shadow thought she seemed calm and composed this morning. There was no sign of any tears.

"How are you feeling today, Lottie?" he asked. "You were very upset last night."

She took a deep breath and brushed a stray hair away from her face. "It was horrible seeing Spencer like that. Lying there so cold and lifeless. I'd only been talking to him in the interval. Do you know what happened?"

"He was poisoned. Someone had switched the bottle of green liquid he drank from."

Her blue eyes opened very wide. "Why? Who would want to kill him?"

"That's what we are trying to find out. We've heard that Mr Knight had made quite a few enemies both in his business and personal life." Shadow watched as Lottie looked down at her hands and started fiddling with the gold signet ring she was wearing on her little finger. "But you didn't feel that way. In fact, I hear you were rather fond of him."

The young woman sighed again and shrugged her shoulders. "I liked him a lot. He was fun and kind. We had some great times together."

Shadow nodded. There was something about the way she

spoke that jarred. He had the feeling that she had been rehearsing the answers she was giving.

"Were the two of you in a relationship?"

She gave another shrug as she looked up. "It wasn't anything serious. He took me to The Star and The Ivy and shopping at Harvey Nics in Leeds a couple of times. He wasn't like the lads at school. He was really interested in helping my career too. He talked about coming down to London with me and getting a place there so I wouldn't have to live in any grotty student digs. He said he'd be able to contact agents for me too." Now those pretty eyes did begin to fill up. "I guess none of that will happen now."

Shadow suspected the tears were real, but possibly more for herself than Spencer.

"Did Spencer ever discuss his other business dealings with you?"

"No, never. I'd have found it boring anyway."

"Did he mention any other girlfriends?"

She gave a small smile and cast her eyes down. "I think there had been quite a few, including Francesca, but he said none of them compared to me."

"Did you see anyone by the prop table who shouldn't have been there last night?"

"Not really, but it was crazy backstage. Everyone was in a panic because Francesca hadn't shown up."

"Was Spencer panicking?"

"No, but then he wasn't the panicking sort. He was always really chilled."

"When did you last see him? I mean, before the performance last night."

"The night before. He came round here so we could go through our lines together one more time," she replied with a coy smile.

"Was it just the two of you?"

"That's right. Dad went out at about seven; that's when Spence arrived. Oh, Rohan was here too, but only for a few minutes. He was checking up on Arthur, wasn't he, sweetheart?" She placed a kiss on the nose of the whippet, who wagged his tail in reply.

"What time did Spencer leave?"

"At about half ten. Dad was due home then."

Shadow nodded, wondering if Stan was aware Spencer had been visiting his daughter behind his back. "All right, that's everything for now. Thank you, Lottie."

He stood up and Jimmy did the same.

"I'll show you out. You stay here, Arthur," she instructed. The whippet obediently sprawled out across the sofa when she moved. The two detectives followed her to the front door.

"You said he was poisoned. What with?" she asked as they stepped outside.

"Methadone. It's a painkiller, a bit like morphine," replied Shadow.

The young woman turned very pale before closing the

door behind them. It was the first time he thought her reaction was genuine.

"What do you think, Chief?" asked Jimmy as they walked back down the street, then immediately launched into his own theory. "Stanley Beresford really didn't like Knight and I think he'd do anything to protect Lottie. Plus, he was in the army, so he's a trained killer."

"He is, and I wouldn't have been surprised if he'd thumped the man he thought was leading his daughter astray, but poisoning? I'm not so sure."

"He could have been the one who put the sabre there."

"He could, but it would be risky. We know he had access to the sabre."

"Maybe he thought if he was the one who noticed it was missing, we wouldn't think it was him who took it. Like a double bluff," Jimmy suggested.

Shadow frowned as he thought about Stanley and Lottie. "Perhaps the sabre was there as an insurance policy in case the poison didn't work but also to detract from the person who had put the poison there. Stanley could have been protecting his daughter, just not the way we think."

Jimmy shook his head as firmly as the collar would allow. "You can't think it was Lottie? She's only a kid."

"She's an intelligent young woman but something she said didn't add up. Her first comment about her relationship with Spencer was that it was nothing serious, but then she contradicted that by saying he was thinking of moving to

London to be with her and said she didn't compare to any of his other girlfriends. Then again, we only have Lottie's word that he made those comments. Spencer could have been ending their relationship and she wanted revenge, or perhaps she realised he was using her in some way."

"I really can't see Lottie as a killer, Chief."

"Maybe not, but speak to their family doctor. Find out if Ann was prescribed methadone before she died."

They were now crossing back over Skeldergate Bridge. Shadow glanced at his watch.

"Isn't it time you were heading to the school?"

"Yes, and I'd better hurry. Are you going back to the station?"

"No, I think I might have a word with the West cousins."

"Really? Even though they were sewn into the horse costume?"

"They might still have seen or heard something."

"Okay, Chief. See you later."

With a wave Jimmy headed down Tower Street while Shadow continued past Clifford's Tower and through the Coppergate shopping centre.

Steven and Matthew West had an office above one of the shops on Shambles. Even on a cold January day, Shadow found himself having to trudge up the ancient street behind a slow-moving party of Chinese tourists. He managed to resist paying a visit to the pie shop below the Wests' office.

Instead, he pushed open the door with the brass plaque that needed polishing and made his way upstairs. The office was every bit as grubby and disorganised as he remembered. Both West cousins were sitting on either side of a desk with their feet up. Steven was reading the newspaper while Matthew was dunking a biscuit into his large mug of tea. He gave a start when he saw Shadow, causing the soggy digestive to drop into the mug with a splash.

"Morning, Chief Inspector. What are you doing here?"

"I came to talk to you about what happened at the pantomime. You both left before I had chance to speak with you last night."

"Sorry about that. It was awful what happened to Spencer, but we were both desperate for a drink and a sit-down." Steven stood up and offered him his chair, but seeing that it was covered in crumbs, Shadow declined.

"Have you been involved with the Ebor Entertainers long?"

"No. This was our first year. We thought it might help with networking," replied Matthew.

"How so?"

"The Ebor Entertainers have always been run by Malcolm and Len. We thought if we got friendly with Len, he might mention us on his radio show, you know, free advertising and all that."

"And then there was Lottie," added Steven.

"What about her?"

"Well, you must have noticed she was the best thing in the pantomime. Everyone is saying she'll be a famous actress one day, so we thought we might be able to talk her into working for us over the Easter and summer holidays, before she goes to drama school. We'd worked out a couple of whole new tours with her playing Margaret Clitherow – 'the pearl of York'."

"She seemed quite keen, but her dad wasn't having any of it. Told us she needed to concentrate on her studies," added Steven.

"Had you met Spencer Knight before taking part in the pantomime?"

The two cousins exchanged a look.

"Actually, we had. He was our financial adviser a couple of years ago."

"And was he a good adviser?"

"He could talk the talk all right. Kept telling us we need to speculate to accumulate."

Shadow frowned. For once he found himself agreeing with Malcolm Webster. He couldn't imagine the Wests' business was so successful that they had much cash to spare for investments. Speculate to accumulate. Wasn't that the mantra of the yuppies Sophie had teased him about?

"He was loaded, always driving around in flash cars, and so we thought he must know what he was talking about. He charged us five grand and promised us all sorts of things like a twenty-four-hour helpline to help us with things like VAT.

We thought that meant we would get to speak to him, but we just got put through to some foreign call centre. They were very nice and everything, but not that much help."

"Five thousand pounds is a lot to lose."

"Too right," agreed Matthew.

"You live and learn," replied Steven.

"If he treated other businesses the way he treated you, he can't have been very popular."

"His type always come up smelling of roses," sighed Matthew.

"He's burnt a few bridges though," added Steven.

"So you won't be surprised to hear he was poisoned last night."

The two of them exchanged another look.

"Poisoned? We thought he'd had a heart attack or a stroke or something," stammered Matthew.

"It was nothing to do with us," added his cousin.

"Is it true you were sewn into your costume throughout the performance?"

"Yes. Malcolm had a fit because the two halves kept coming apart and flapping around in rehearsals, so about ten minutes before curtains up Susan sewed it together and the idea was to cut the stitches at the last curtain call, not that we made it that far. Susan buggered off too, so Rohan ended up cutting us out instead."

"It doesn't sound very comfortable."

"It was a nightmare. I didn't think I'd make it through

the dress rehearsal."

"On the plus side, you sweat loads. It's like being in a sauna. I reckon if I'd done it for both nights, I would have lost about half a stone."

Steven, the thinner cousin, wrinkled his face in disgust.

"You'd put it on again with all the beer you pour down your throat!"

Shadow didn't want to dwell on the two of them perspiring in a pantomime horse.

"Did you notice anything unusual before the performance or during the interval?"

Both men shook their heads.

"No. We were running late and when we arrived everyone was in a bit of a panic about Francesca not turning up," said Steven.

"Except Spencer," added Matthew. "He kept saying there was nothing to worry about and she'd show up in time. We got into costume and that was it. I'm the back end so I couldn't see a thing except Steve's arse."

"The holes I look through aren't very big, so I could only see what is directly in front of me."

"And you shared your dressing room with Rohan Kapoor?"

"Yep. Us NSPs weren't important enough to have individual dressing rooms."

"NSPs?"

"Non-Speaking Parts, Chief Inspector."

"I see. Well, thank you for your time, and if you do think of anything else, let me know."

As he left the Wests' office and stepped on to the Shambles, he could hear the Minster bells striking twelve. Lunchtime. It was hopeless. He couldn't resist the delicious aroma coming from the pie shop any longer. As he waited in the queue, he decided to call an old friend and hope it was his lunch break too.

Warm pork pie in hand, he munched away as he headed across King's Square towards Goodramgate. Unfortunately, his enjoyment was spoilt by a figure in a black cape and hat heading towards him.

"Ah, Chief Inspector Shadow! Being hot on the heels of a poisoner hasn't dampened your appetite I see!" said Malcolm loudly, causing several tourists to stop and stare. Shadow scowled and brushed the pastry crumbs from his mouth.

"How did you know Spencer was poisoned?" he asked quietly, feeling like a piece of street theatre.

"I've just spoken to Susan. She was most upset with you. Said you practically evicted her from Spencer's place."

"You don't seem very surprised that your leading man was murdered."

"I'm not. As I told you last night, Spencer had ruffled plenty of feathers both personally and professionally."

"Did you ever go to him for business advice?"

"Never. I only met him when he joined the Ebor Entertainers."

"And when was that?"

"About six months ago. Francesca had been with us from the start. Her husband was often away, and she liked to keep herself busy. That's before she left said husband for Spencer. She talked him into coming along too. Then I'm sure she regretted it. Once he met Lottie, poor Francesca rather faded into the background. But who could blame him? Lottie is quite the star. I doubt the Ebor Entertainers will be blessed with a talent like hers again. It was on the strength of her performance that I managed to get us into the Theatre Royal for two nights. We usually put our shows on at the Friargate Theatre. It's such a shame we can't finish our run. I did consider taking the role of Prince Charming myself – the show must go on and all that – but Susan and Len thought it would be in bad taste."

Shadow managed to stop himself laughing out loud at the thought of Webster trying to woo the beautiful, young Snow White.

"Did you go backstage during the interval?" he asked instead.

"Sadly not. I was far too occupied with the gentlemen of the press. They were all clamouring for a quote from the director of the production."

Shadow nodded. Malcolm's version of events wasn't quite the same as Tom's.

"I see, well, thank you for your help."

"Not at all, Chief Inspector, and never fear: the Ebor Entertainers shall rise again and I'll be sure you get tickets to our next production. Front row this time."

Shadow walked away, shuddering at the thought. A few moments later, his progress was impeded again. Outside the Cross Keys, he found himself fighting through a throng of excited students in their gowns and mortar boards accompanied by proud, beaming parents. Inside, the pub was filled with them too. Luckily George had managed to claim a table in the window and had already got the drinks in. Another thing Shadow had missed while he was in Italy was a decent pint. He sat down and raised his glass of Black Sheep.

"A belated Happy New Year, George."

"To you too," replied his old friend. "I wasn't sure if I'd be seeing you again. There was a rumour you might stay in Italy."

"So I hear." He nodded to the crowd of students. "Graduation ceremony at the Minster, I take it?"

"They're on all week. I've been rushed off my feet," grumbled George, who since retiring had taken up a part-time job as one of the Minster police.

"I know the feeling."

"You've got a case already? Funnily enough, I didn't think you'd phoned just to be sociable."

Shadow gave a wry smile. "Someone was poisoned at the Ebor Entertainers' pantomime last night."

George raised an eyebrow. "I heard something about that, but assumed it was a joke."

Shadow shook his head. "It was the leading man, Spencer Knight."

"Good riddance to bad rubbish."

Shadow looked up in surprise. It was unlike George to react so harshly.

"You know him?"

George took a sip of beer. His usually open and friendly face had darkened.

"Unfortunately, yes. When Kate was a student, she did a couple of weeks' work experience for Mr Spencer. She was young and impressionable, and he turned on the charm. One thing led to another, and, well, she thought he was the best thing since sliced bread, but he finished with her after a couple of weeks. She was heartbroken. Now, this all happened at the same time Carol's mum died. She'd left everything to Carol. It came to about a hundred grand, and Kate must have told Knight about it. He came round to ours to pick Kate up one night with flowers for Carol, a bottle of Scotch for me and enough flannel to wash an elephant. Started telling us about this investment scheme and timeshares in Spain; made out like we couldn't lose. I told him straight: the money was going to pay off our mortgage. The next day Kate was dumped."

He took a sip of his pint and shook his head. "It was all a long time ago. Kate's happy and married with kids now, but no father likes to see his daughter taken advantage of and hurt. From what I heard she wasn't the only one."

Shadow nodded as his thoughts drifted back to Stanley and Lottie.

"Did his behaviour ever lead to anything we got involved in? Any fights with disgruntled husbands or fathers? Any complaints from anyone who did take him up on his investment advice?"

George frowned for a moment, then shook his head. "Not that I recall. I'm sure there were plenty who would have liked to thump that smug grin off his face, but I would have remembered if he'd been involved in any assaults." He paused again. "There was something though. We were called out, not by him but by one of his neighbours. A woman was outside in the car park shouting and screaming, pressing the intercom and demanding to be let in. Apparently, Knight was inside with the woman in question's replacement."

"What happened?"

"When a couple of our lads arrived, they found the spurned woman was taking a sharp rock to the paintwork of his flash sports car. Spencer was furious apparently but tried to keep things quiet. He didn't want any bad publicity. I think she was cautioned though."

"What was her name?"

"Sorry, John. I can't remember. It happened when I was on holiday; I heard about it when I got back. I was only interested because it involved him."

Shadow was making a mental note to get Tom to check the records as soon as he got back to the station when they were interrupted by a loud tapping on the window. They both turned to find Jimmy looking back at them through the glass. He pointed to Shadow, then pointed over his shoulder. In return, Shadow scowled and pointed to his pint that was still half full. Jimmy then began a series of dramatic gestures, starting with drawing a finger across his neck, pointing at his watch and ending with an exaggerated mime of turning an imaginary steering wheel.

"Duty calls by the look of things," said George with a grin. "Sergeant Chang is certainly animated when he wants to be, isn't he?"

"He's spent too much time at the theatre with those amateur actors," muttered Shadow. "It's his fault I was at the pantomime in the first place." He threw back the rest of his pint, shook George by the hand and then pushed his way out into the street.

Chapter Five

Down 3 (9 letters)
One MD uses heat to make an opioid

"As usual, your timing is perfect. Couldn't you have waited until I finished my pint?" he complained to Jimmy, who was standing next one of the pool cars with the hazard lights flashing.

"Sorry, Chief, but a body has been found. It's Francesca French. Spencer Knight's partner."

"How was she killed?" asked Shadow as he climbed into the passenger seat and Jimmy slowly and awkwardly got behind the wheel.

"Stabbed, Chief. Actually, that's a bit of an understatement. Sophie's already there. She phoned me and said she was killed by a single wound to the abdomen. It went right through her. Soph said it was like she'd been skewered. Like a kebab."

"Your wife certainly has a way with words. Any sign of the weapon?"

"Not yet, Chief."

"And where was she found?"

"At the cottage she'd just bought at Sutton on the Forest."

"Let's go then."

As they drove along, Shadow updated Jimmy on the conversations he'd had with the Wests, Malcolm and George.

"So you think we can rule out the West cousins and Mr Webster?" he asked.

"I think so. I can't see how Matthew and Steven had the opportunity and five thousand pounds might be a lot for them to lose, but not worth killing someone, I'd say. And for once I'm inclined to believe Malcolm. Mr Knight may not have been the most honest of businessmen, but I don't think he was stupid. He wouldn't have targeted Malcolm for one of his scams."

"You mean because Malcolm hasn't got much money?" asked Jimmy.

"I mean because he's in a relationship with the sister of the county's chief constable, who might start asking awkward questions if Malcolm was to lose whatever cash he may or may not have. What about you? Did any of the dwarves have much to say?"

"Plenty, but I'm not sure if any of it was very useful, and I still need to interview one of them who was off sick. Kitty, the little girl who Angela had to take home last night. I'll put their statements on your desk when I've got them typed up."

"I'll look forward to it," replied Shadow without any

conviction.

∽

Sutton on the Forest was a village about eight miles to the north of York. Francesca's cottage was on the edge of the village, halfway down a single-track lane. When they arrived at the scene, it was already swarming with uniformed and scenes-of-crime officers. Shadow and Jimmy stepped out of the car, pulled on their protective suits and gloves, and crossed the police tape that had sealed off the area.

"Who found the body?" asked Shadow.

"A man who works for the estate agents. The sale had only gone through a few days ago. He came this morning to take away the 'for sale' board and found her. Poor guy. Apparently, he's thrown up at least twice," explained Jimmy, pointing to a pale-faced young man crouched next to a police car with a uniformed officer by his side holding a towel.

Shadow's heart sank. Even after all these years in CID, he was still incredibly squeamish and very much hoped he wouldn't be joining the unfortunate young man. They walked up the drive where an Audi was parked in front of the garage.

"We've already checked, and it's registered to Francesca French," supplied Jimmy as he opened the small wooden garden gate. There was a thin brick path that led up to the cottage. It was built of stone with sash windows and a white painted front door that even had roses growing around it. Shadow imagined it was the sort of property estate agents dreamt of.

"Nice place," he commented.

"Yes, it's really pretty," agreed Jimmy. "Unfortunately, Francesca never made it inside."

Shadow turned to where his sergeant was pointing. At the bottom of the garden, Sophie was standing next to the body, currently covered by a plastic sheet. She greeted them both with a cheerful wave.

"Hello again. Hey, Jimmy was right – you have got a suntan. I couldn't tell last night under the bright stage lights. It suits you."

"Thanks," grunted Shadow. He had a feeling tan or no tan, all the colour was about to drain out of his face. "Let's get it over with then," he said with a nod towards the body on the ground. Sophie and Jimmy obligingly turned back the sheet. Beneath was a woman of about forty. Her brown hair was loosely curled, the make-up on her face had been carefully and subtly applied and she was wearing high-heeled black ankle boots and a black leather jacket. Shadow was relieved that the only visible evidence of her murder was a dark red stain around the tear in the middle of her animal-print mini dress.

"She was killed with a single stab wound. They attacked her from behind but it went right through. That's the exit wound her at the front. They weren't messing about. It's so precise you could say it's the work of a professional. Whoever killed her must have used some force. My guess is they completely severed the spinal cord."

Shadow grimaced and swallowed down the bile he could feel rising in his throat.

"Are you saying the killer was a man?"

"Or a strong, fit woman. They had the strength to drag her over here too. She was actually killed closer to the path. There's a trail of blood over the grass."

"Why would they move her?" asked Jimmy.

"To try to hide her, I think. The road that runs alongside this hedge is pretty quiet, but if a tractor was driving by, I bet the driver would be high enough to see over into the garden," replied Sophie, who had grown up on a farm. "They would have spotted the body if she had been left where she was killed, but not down here. The guy who found her didn't even notice at first. It was only when he spotted the stuff she'd dropped." She pointed to where a handbag and a few other items were scattered in the long grass.

"Any thoughts on the time of death?"

"It's tricky as the temperature has been below freezing for the last couple of days but I'd say she's been here for about forty-eight hours. Look, an animal has had a nibble at her hand." She pointed to small teeth marks on the edge of Francesca's palm. "My guess is she was killed on Sunday, but

I'll be able to give you a better idea after the post-mortem."

Shadow took a deep breath and raised his hand to his mouth.

"But you think it was before Knight was killed?"

"Oh, definitely."

"Any thoughts on the weapon?"

"Well, something with a long blade – at least two feet – and about an inch wide.

Shadow exchanged a look with Jimmy.

"That sounds very much like our sabre."

"The ceremonial one that was stolen and then turned up at the theatre?" asked Sophie.

Shadow nodded. "Where is it now?" he asked.

"Ben and Ollie have it," replied Jimmy.

"And where are they? I thought they would have been here by now."

"They're at the hospital. They're both getting their collars taken off today."

"Pity it wasn't before all this started," grumbled Shadow. "How long will they be?"

Jimmy checked his phone. "They're about to set off now. Shall I ask them to bring the sabre with them?"

"Will it help you, Sophie?" asked Shadow.

Sophie shook her head. "I'd rather take a look after I've examined her properly. Am I okay to the move the body now?"

Shadow nodded, and he and Jimmy stood to one side as

the dead woman was carefully placed on a stretcher and taken to the waiting private ambulance.

"If it turns out the stolen sabre really was the murder weapon, that means it was stolen on Saturday night, used to kill Francesca sometime on Sunday, then found its way backstage at the theatre in time for Monday night's performance of the pantomime," mused Jimmy.

Shadow frowned. "It's what, about three feet long in total? You can't exactly slip it into your pocket. Surely someone must have spotted it being carried around."

"How about if it was stolen and taken to the theatre with the idea of killing Spencer, but someone found it and used it to kill Francesca and then returned it to the theatre?" suggested Jimmy.

"It still doesn't explain how it was moved around without anyone noticing."

Taking care where he placed his feet, he walked back towards the cottage and the collection of the dead woman's belongings. Lying next to the garden path, partly hidden in the grass, was a small leather handbag, a set of keys and bottle of champagne.

"She'd come here to celebrate," he said.

"Getting the keys to the cottage maybe," suggested Jimmy.

Shadow knelt down and carefully opened the bag and looked inside.

"There's her phone, purse and car keys." He handed the

phone to Jimmy. "Can you turn it on?"

His sergeant pressed a couple of buttons then shook his head. "Sorry, Chief, no. The battery is dead. I'll get Ben and Ollie to take a look though."

He slipped the phone into an evidence bag while Shadow opened the purse. "All credit cards and about forty pounds still here."

"And they didn't take her car, so theft wasn't the motive. Unless they dropped the house keys back here again, it doesn't look like they were interested in anything that could be inside either."

Shadow picked up the keys that were still attached to the keyring bearing the estate agent's logo.

"Let's take a look for ourselves."

He turned the key in the lock and the door opened with a creak. He tried the light switch but nothing happened. "When did she buy the place?" he asked.

Jimmy consulted his notebook again. "The estate agents said the sale completed on Friday and that it had been empty for a few months. The previous owner died. I guess Francesca didn't have time to get the electricity reconnected."

They made their way through the rooms in semi-darkness. All carpets and curtains had been removed and there were no electrical appliances in the kitchen, but in the largest of the two upstairs bedrooms several big brightly coloured cushions had been scattered on the floor along with a faux fur throw. In the little fireplace there were half a dozen thick white candles waiting to be lit, and a pair of champagne flutes were on the hearth stone.

"Looks like she was planning on meeting up with someone here. Spencer, do you think?" asked Jimmy.

"Maybe. The question is, did whoever she arranged all this for turn up, and did they kill her?"

"Do you think Spencer could have killed Francesca and then he was killed by someone who had found out what he'd done?"

"Two murderers? It seems unlikely, but it might explain the plethora of suspects," he said almost to himself. "Get the place checked for fingerprints, particularly Spencer's, and tell Ben and Ollie to make accessing Francesca's phone a priority." Then as an afterthought: "Once they have found out if that damn sabre is our murder weapon."

The two of them left the crime scene team to their work and returned to the station. They were about to head up to the incident room when the desk sergeant called out to them. "Chief Inspector, the media team at Northallerton left you a message. Word has got out about a second suspected murder and the local press have been in touch with them. They want to talk to you about issuing a statement."

Shadow frowned. The media team or press office, as they used to be called, were based at North Yorkshire Police's headquarters and were the bane of his life during an investigation.

"Phone them back and tell them not to issue anything.

The victim's next of kin haven't been informed yet."

The sergeant nodded then turned to Jimmy. "Your sister is waiting for you in one of the interview rooms, Sarge, and so is a Mr Kapoor."

"Oh, that's right," replied Jimmy. "Angela said she and Rohan would be coming over to make their witness statements together after school. Rohan wasn't sure where the station was, and I think he was a bit nervous."

"I'll take their statements," said Shadow. "You go and find out who Francesca's next of kin is and keep chasing forensics and check on finance."

He made his way to the rear of the Guildhall and found Angela and Rohan sitting side by side in the corridor outside one of the interview rooms.

"Thank you both for coming. Angela, I'll speak with you first if I may."

He opened the door of the interview room and ushered her in. They both took a seat on either side of the large table overlooking the swirling brown river below. Shadow rummaged through his pockets for his old notebook and pen. He couldn't remember the last time he'd used it. He'd grown reliant on Jimmy and his electronic gadgets.

"How are the children? Not too troubled by what happened, I hope," he began, giving the biro a shake and hoping it still worked. Angela gave a smile and shook her head.

"Not at all. If anything, they seemed to find the whole thing quite exciting, apart from Kitty, the girl I took home;

she's a sensitive little soul. She didn't come into school today. As for the others, I think they were a bit disappointed that Jimmy didn't slap them in handcuffs."

"Well, they are meant to be very resilient," replied Shadow, although in truth he had very little experience of children. "What can you tell me about last night? What time did you arrive at the theatre?"

"I got there at about five thirty. Stan and Susan were already there. I helped Susan make sure the costumes for the children were in order and as they arrived got them changed in the large dressing room. The rest of the cast filtered in over the next half hour or so, I think."

"Except Francesca French."

"Yes, but nobody was worried at first. She was often the last to turn up for rehearsals. She liked to make an entrance."

Shadow stopped scribbling for a second and cleared his throat.

"I'm sorry to have to tell you that Francesca has also been killed."

Angela's hand flew to her mouth. "Oh my goodness. That's terrible. Do you think it's the same person who killed Spencer?"

"That's what we are trying to find out."

Angela shifted in her chair. "Now I feel bad for saying she liked making an entrance, even if it was true."

Shadow looked down at the notes he was making and smiled to himself. He'd never known Angela be anything but completely honest.

"Who was last to arrive last night?" he asked.

"Spencer. He had just turned up when you saw him backstage."

"Did everyone have their own dressing room?"

"Rohan shared with the two West boys, and the children shared the largest dressing room, but everyone else did, yes. I used Francesca's when I knew I would be playing her part."

"Who was the first to notice Francesca was missing?"

Angela frowned. "I think it was Susan. She was in charge of costumes and props. I remember her knocking on the door and asking if I'd seen her. When I said I hadn't, she tutted and said, 'Typical, she isn't answering her phone either,' then went to find Malcolm and tell him. After she'd gone, I tried phoning Francesca myself, in case she just didn't want to speak to Susan, but there was no reply."

Shadow nodded. He didn't tell her that it wouldn't have mattered who had called as Francesca was already dead. Instead, he asked, "Susan and Francesca didn't get on?"

"Not really. They were jealous of each other, well, they were jealous of anyone they thought was close to Spencer."

"So, Lottie can't have been very popular with either of them."

"Susan was always polite to her, if a bit cold, but Francesca barely spoke to the poor girl."

"Is it true that Francesca wanted the part of Snow White?"

"Yes, I think she had this romantic idea that Spencer would commit to her if they fell in love onstage. For an intelligent woman, she was very silly where he was concerned."

"Did you see or hear anything strange that night? Anyone hanging around the prop table who shouldn't have been there?"

"I'm sorry but no, I didn't. It was all so chaotic. Whenever I was offstage, I was running through my lines and trying to keep an eye on the children too. Rohan was doing his best to help with them. He's got DBS clearance from when he helped out at a petting zoo, so I was happy to leave them with him, otherwise we would have needed to ask Tom, and he was busy videoing up with the Dawsons. Oh, and Susan helped too. She knew some of the children from when she worked at the school. With all that on my mind, I really didn't notice what anyone else was doing."

Shadow nodded. She was confirming what Susan had told them.

"Thank you, Angela. I'll get someone to type this up and Jimmy or someone will get you to sign it," he told her a little uncertainly. In truth, he couldn't quite remember the procedure for witness statements. They usually just appeared on his desk.

He showed Angela out, and she gave Rohan a reassuring smile before he took her place opposite Shadow. The young man looked nervous as he adjusted his glasses. He was wearing a very long raincoat that went almost to his ankles. When he removed it to sit down, he was dressed casually in a University of Edinburgh sweatshirt and jeans that he self-consciously brushed dog hairs from. As he arranged his tall, skinny frame, he reminded Shadow of his sergeant.

"Thank you for coming to make a statement," he began. "I understand you work for a local vet."

"Yes. I'm an international student. I left India to study at Edinburgh and now I'm doing my master's in veterinary medicine at Bishop Askham," he explained.

Shadow nodded. He was vaguely aware of the large agricultural college a few miles out of the city.

"I moved to York in September," continued Rohan. "I'm on a six-month placement at Town and County Vets. It's part of my degree course, but I graduate soon, then I'm going to Brazil to volunteer at an animal sanctuary there for a year. I'm currently living in the flat above the practice if you need my address."

"How did you come to be involved in the pantomime? Have you acted before?"

The young man looked embarrassed and shook his head. "No, not at all. I don't even like public speaking usually, but I got to know Lottie when I helped treat Arthur, her dog, or at least he's the dog she and her dad look after, and she suggested I go along. When I got there, Malcolm offered me the part of the evil queen's henchman. He said I didn't have to say anything, just look tough and fierce."

Shadow thought Rohan had looked more worried and confused, like a man who'd remembered he hadn't locked his front door, when he was onstage. As if reading his mind, the young man continued: "I don't think I was very convincing, but Lottie knew I didn't know many people in York and said it would be a good way to meet people."

"And was it?"

"Yes, I suppose so. I like to think Angela and Tom have become friends, and Steve and Matt too. Len is a pretty funny guy. Every Wednesday after rehearsals we'd all go for a drink, not that I drink, but it was nice to be included."

"What about Spencer Knight and Francesca French?"

"To be honest, I didn't really speak to Francesca much. She seemed to be in a bad mood a lot of the time."

"And Spencer Knight?"

Rohan shrugged. "He was friendly enough but spent most of the time talking to Lottie."

"Did that bother you at all?"

Rohan frowned and fiddled with his glasses again. "Do you mean was I jealous, Chief Inspector?"

"Lottie is a very attractive young lady."

The young man seemed embarrassed. "She is and a good friend, but that's all. Even if I had wanted more, she wasn't interested in me, and as I said, I leave for South America soon."

"Can you tell us what happened on Monday night before Spencer collapsed?"

"We all got there about six like Malcolm had asked, except Francesca of course and Spencer wasn't there either, but he was often late. Malcolm gave us a bit of a pep talk, and we all started getting into costume. Then about five minutes before the curtain was due to go up, we realised Angela was going to have to go on instead of Francesca. That's when everything got a bit manic. It meant Susan and I were going to have to help look after the children when Angela was onstage. I didn't mind – they are nice kids – but between you and me, I don't think Susan likes children much. She was quite cross when she was left on her own with them."

"When you and Angela were onstage?"

"Yes, and when I was offstage, I often had to help Stan move some of the bigger bits of scenery too."

"So you didn't help Susan with putting out the props at all?"

"No, that was definitely her domain. She was quite protective about it, kept shooing away the children if they tried to help."

"Did you see her putting out the bottle of green liquid or the swords you were due to fight with?"

"No, I was too busy."

"I understand you were due to take part in a sword fight with Spencer in the second half."

"Yes, that's right. Malcolm called it 'my moment', but I was pretty nervous about it."

"And you were to collect your sword from the prop table?"

"Yes, I was meant to attack Snow White then the prince, I mean Spencer, came to her rescue."

"Were the swords different?"

"Yes, mine was straight and Spencer's was curved. Malcolm gave us a long lecture about how it was what a cavalry officer would have used. Originally, Spencer was meant to arrive on horseback. There was talk of getting a real horse, then using Dobbin the pantomime horse, but Steve and Matt weren't keen on that idea." He gave a half smile. "Like much of this production, it all got a bit complicated in the end."

Shadow nodded. He could quite imagine Malcolm's grandiose schemes coming to nothing.

"Would the rest of the cast know who would have used which sword?" he asked.

Rohan shrugged. "I think so."

Shadow frowned. If that was the case, then it would mean whoever put the stolen sabre on the table meant Spencer to use it. Surely Rohan couldn't have been the intended victim. The young man was watching him expectantly.

"What was the outcome of the fight meant to be?" asked Shadow.

"Oh, Spencer killed me," he replied cheerfully. "That's what I was worried about – falling properly. There's this way Malcolm and Len showed me where you drop to your knees then flop on to your side, but I kept messing it up. I think it's my height."

Shadow nodded. "I'm afraid we have more bad news. Francesca French was found dead earlier today."

The young man blinked several times before replying. "I'm sorry to hear that, Chief Inspector. I didn't know her well, but still…"

"We believe she may have been killed with the sabre we discovered at the theatre last night."

"The sabre that was missing after the regimental dinner?"

"You know about that?"

"Yes, Stan told me. He thought I might be interested. I had collected him and Arthur after the dinner, you see."

"Why was that?"

"Well, Arthur shouldn't have been there really. He's meant to be recovering after his operation, but the major said it wouldn't be the same without him. I didn't really understand why, but it's tradition apparently. The major told me the story of the Marquess of Granby and how he made sure those he'd served with were taken care of. It reminded me a little of an uncle of mine who was also a very generous man." Shadow nodded along thinking Rohan was as talkative as Jimmy too. "Anyway, even though Arthur wasn't a hundred per cent, Stan didn't want to disappoint the major. So, Arthur went, but was kept in his crate, so he couldn't move about too much and risk damaging his stitches. The crate needs two people to carry it and only fits in the back of a van or estate car, so I helped Stan take him and we both picked him up again using the practice's Volvo. I was on call that evening anyway."

Shadow scribbled all this down, thinking it seemed like an awful lot of trouble for one whippet.

"Did you see the sabre when you were there or notice anything unusual?"

Rohan shook his head. "No, not really, but then I was only focused on taking care of Arthur. Everyone did seem quite merry by the end of the evening."

Shadow smiled to himself at the young man's quaint way of phrasing what had clearly been a night of heavy drinking. Rohan sighed and shook his head.

"It doesn't make sense, Chief Inspector. If you are correct and I'm sure you are," he added quickly, "then someone stole the sabre, used it to kill Francesca, then left it at the theatre where it was bound to be found. Don't murderers usually try to get rid of the weapon they have used?"

"Usually," agreed Shadow.

"Then there must a reason they allowed it to be found so easily," reasoned Rohan.

"Do you think Spencer would have realised it was a real sword when he picked it up?"

"Probably, although he would have been in a rush." The young man paused and looked thoughtful. "I hope for my sake he would."

"You don't think there is any chance you could have

been the intended victim?"

Rohan seemed amused by the idea. "No," he replied, shaking his head. "Who would want to kill me? I barely know anyone here. Besides Spencer is the one who died. Maybe someone didn't know about the difference between the swords and thought I could do their dirty work if whatever they poisoned him with didn't work. That would make more sense."

Shadow was inclined to agree with him, at least for now. He stood up and shook the young man's hand.

"Thank you again. I'll be in touch if I have any more questions."

Rohan stood up, looking visibly relieved. He was almost out of the door when Shadow remembered something.

"By the way, you know Major Armitage. Did you happen to see him at the theatre last night?"

Rohan turned back and nodded. "Yes. I passed him in the corridor before the performance started when I went to look for my script. He was arguing with Malcolm, who wouldn't let him come backstage. Malcolm is very strict about us not being seen in costume and 'civilians' – as he puts it – coming backstage."

"Why would the major want to go backstage?"

Rohan shrugged. "To see Francesca, I imagine. He must have thought she would be there." Then noticing Shadow's confused expression: "She's his wife, or at least was. They are separated or getting divorced or something."

With that he raised his hand, gave another half-smile and left. Shadow thought for a second about what he'd learnt, then picked up his notebook and made his way to the incident room.

Chapter Six

Across 8 (4 letters)
A vole to adore

"Francesca French was married to Major Armitage," he announced as he walked through the door at the same time Jimmy was finishing a telephone call.

"Yes, Chief," his sergeant replied. "I've just found out too. Their decree absolute was granted at the beginning of last week. How did you know?"

"Rohan told me."

"He's a nice guy, isn't he? And really clever. He fixed Mum's computer while I was away."

Shadow tutted impatiently. "He also said he saw the major trying to get backstage but Malcolm stopped him."

"Do you think he could have got through anyway?"

"Possibly. If he did, surely someone would have seen him. Neither Stanley nor Lottie mentioned his connection to Francesca when we spoke to them either. Even after we told them we'd found the sabre."

"Maybe they thought we knew or didn't think it was important. They didn't know she was dead at the time. It explains why the major was at the theatre and why he left. He must have wanted to see Francesca and by the interval, he realised she wasn't there. Do you think he's involved?"

Shadow was silent for a moment as he considered the question. "We know Francesca was killed before the pantomime. If the major was responsible, he might still turn up and act as though he wanted to see her, to avoid suspicion. But, if the sabre does turn out to be our murder weapon, why risk keeping it and leaving it at the theatre?"

"Unless he thought it could be used to kill Spencer too during the fight scene. Or maybe he'd taken it to the theatre earlier and wanted to get it back, and that's why he wanted to get backstage."

Shadow shook his head impatiently. "But Spencer was killed with methadone. We need to find out if the major could have got hold of any. And according to Rohan, it would have been Spencer using the sabre, not him."

"The major might not have known that. Or maybe he isn't involved. Or he is involved, but he's working with someone else. Or there are two completely separate killers. What do you think?"

"I think as usual we have too many questions and not enough answers. Let's pay a visit to the major and see if he can provide some."

THEY FOUND MAJOR Armitage at his office in the regimental headquarters. He didn't appear particularly surprised to see them.

"I thought I might be seeing you gentlemen again. Is this about Spencer Knight?" he asked as he stood up to shake their hands.

"Partly," replied Shadow, "but we also have some news regarding your ex-wife. Perhaps you would like to sit down again, Major."

"I hope you don't think she was involved in this business. Spencer had plenty of enemies, but Francesca wasn't one of them, unfortunately."

"I'm sorry to have to tell you that Francesca is dead. Her body was discovered earlier today."

The major stared at Shadow in bewilderment. "What do you mean dead? She can't be. How?"

"We believe she has been murdered. Is there anyone you would like us to contact? Do the two of you have any children?"

He didn't reply at first and Shadow wondered if he'd heard him. His ramrod-straight frame was now slumped in the chair. He began to shake his head.

"No children. Francesca never wanted any. Didn't really like them. She never even wanted any pets either. Wanted to focus on her career. She worked for a bank before she became a financial adviser. It was just the two of us; that was enough. At least I thought it was."

"I understand your divorce was finalised last week. May I ask if the separation was a joint decision?"

"No, it was Francesca's idea. Not that I blame her. I was away an awful lot. She must have found it lonely. Then she met Knight at the golf club. The two of them started working together and…" He trailed off.

"Did you know Mr Knight?"

The major straightened himself and raised his head. "Yes, I knew the man. He was a common thief, nothing more. Whatever he wanted to acquire, he stole. Whether it was a business owner's hard-earned profits or another man's wife."

"We believe Francesca may have been killed with the sabre you reported missing."

"Good God! Who could have done such a thing?" He looked first at Shadow and then at Jimmy. "You don't think it was me, do you? I wouldn't hurt Francesca for the world."

"We found the sabre at the theatre yesterday evening after Spencer Knight collapsed and died. You were at the theatre but left during the interval."

"Yes, I'd gone to see Francesca. To support her."

"Even though you were no longer married?"

"Yes. A bit of paper didn't mean I'd stopped caring about her. I only wanted to wish her good luck but that buffoon Webster wouldn't let me. He insisted it wasn't allowed. If he had simply told me she wasn't there, I could have come home."

"Do you live here, Major Armitage?"

"Yes. For the time being. The house, our family home, was sold as part of the divorce."

"Where did your wife live?"

"She'd been renting a flat in a street off Bishopthorpe Road and was in the process of buying a cottage out in the sticks somewhere."

"She never moved in with Spencer?"

"No, although I believe she was trying to persuade him to join her in her new place. Fat chance."

"You don't think it was likely?"

The major's expression turned scornful. "Spencer give up his plush pad to live in the middle of nowhere? Of course that's the very reason she bought it. To keep him away from temptation. No, I'm afraid Francesca was deluding herself."

"Can I ask you about your movements over the weekend?"

"Is that when it happened? Good God. No wonder she wasn't at the theatre."

"Sir, the weekend," pressed Shadow.

"All Saturday I was here preparing for the regimental dinner. I never left. On Sunday, I woke up about lunchtime with one hell of a hangover and made myself a full English, then played a round of golf to try to clear my head. Had a few hairs of the dog at the clubhouse, then came back here."

"At what time?" asked Shadow, noting the large golf bag in the corner of the room.

"I don't remember. Nine-ish. The news was coming on

when I turned on the radio."

"Can anyone confirm that?"

"I'm afraid not, but as I said, I wouldn't hurt my wife for the world, and I wouldn't be foolish enough to use a sword I'd just told the police had been stolen. I assume I don't need to account for my movements on Monday, as much of the time I was talking to you or your colleagues."

Shadow decided to try another tack. "Aside from members of the regiment, who else was here for the dinner? Did you have outside caterers?"

"Yes, Chrissie, who incidentally runs the golf club restaurant, has a catering company. She and her team were here. I think there were about four or five of them, mainly youngsters. Oh, and that young vet chap came to help Stan with Arthur. It's all due to cutbacks, I'm afraid. At one time the army would have always used the catering corps and had their own vets on hand too."

"Were officers allowed to bring their partners?" asked Shadow.

"No. More cost-cutting by the MOD, sadly. They always used to be invited. I think that was the only part of me being in the army that Francesca enjoyed. She always liked getting dressed up." His voice cracked a little as he spoke, and he quickly began to make a show of rearranging the already neat papers on his desk.

Shadow gave Jimmy a brisk nod and they both rose to their feet.

"That's all for now, thank you, Major Armitage. We'll be in touch if we have any further information, but please let us know if you are planning on leaving the area." The major nodded silently and remained seated. The two detectives left him alone and showed themselves out.

"He seemed genuine enough, Chief," said Jimmy as the gates clanged shut behind them.

"He did, but still check his bank account. See how the divorce was going to leave him financially. And speak to the golf club. See if anyone saw him on Sunday and find out if it was the same club where Spencer supposedly left his laptop."

"Do you think the two of them could have been there at the same time? Had an argument maybe?"

"Perhaps," replied Shadow as he waited impatiently for his sergeant to put on his hat, scarf and gloves, "but it also strikes me that a golf bag would be about the right size to carry a sabre. We should probably speak to this Chrissie, the catering person, and keep chasing all the other officers who were at the dinner. See if any of them have video footage of the night. I want to try to pinpoint exactly when the sabre was taken."

"I was thinking, I might not have to contact them directly. They might have posted on social media. I could take a look as soon as we get back to the station," said Jimmy through chattering teeth.

"All right, all right. We're heading back there now," he replied. "I'm still amazed you went skiing on your honeymoon when you hate the cold so much."

"It's different out there. Not so damp. Besides it's what Sophie wanted." His phone pinged and he checked the screen. "It's Jane from finance. Apparently, they've spent a lot of time having to field calls from disgruntled clients and are still analysing the information on the computers but are going to email you Spencer's contact list over." Then seeing Shadow's frowning face: "I'll get Tom to print it out and leave it on your desk."

When they returned to the station, Jimmy immediately found a seat near the warmest radiator and began trawling through Facebook, Instagram and TikTok.

Shadow returned to his office where Tom had obligingly left the list of Spencer Knight's contacts for him. His eyes travelled down the list. He knew plenty of the names but two in particular stuck out: Maggie and Cornelius Rutherford. Cornelius was one of the city's most well-respected solicitors. His family's firm had been dealing with the citizens of York's wills, divorces and house purchases for almost two centuries. Shadow picked up the phone and called him. Cornelius's secretary put him through immediately.

"Ah, Shadow! I heard you had returned to us. What's this about? Spencer Knight?" asked the solicitor cheerfully.

"We found your name on his phone. Were you a client of his or was it the other way around?"

"Very much the latter. Not sure I would even trust him with my grandson's pocket money."

"Was he as dodgy as everyone tells me?"

"As far as I am aware he operated within the confines of the law."

"But?"

"Let's just say, I'm pleased I am not required to make a moral judgement when it comes to some of my clients. Spencer Knight set up companies and closed them as frequently as you and I might order a whisky or in your case a wine. He had no compunction about dissolving one of his businesses, regardless of how it affected his creditors. Not only in this country either. Businesses throughout Europe and indeed further afield were substantially out of pocket thanks to him. He also managed to inherit several substantial sums from…how shall I put it? Lonely old ladies. Grateful clients he called them."

Shadow grunted. The more he learnt about Mr Knight the less he liked him.

"Did he leave a will?"

"Yes, I'm the executor. I'll be applying for probate over the next day or two."

"Who inherits?"

"Nobody."

"What?"

"No living family. I vaguely recall his mother dying a few years ago. Spencer was too busy to attend her funeral but managed to turn up for the reading of the will. And before you ask, none of his many lady friends are named either. In fact, I believe he only made the will in the first place because he was pursuing one of our young female solicitors at the time and insisted she drew it up."

"What happens to his money?"

"If memory serves, he made some outlandish declaration that 'if there is anything left, and I sincerely hope there isn't, I want a bloody big statue of my likeness erected next to the eighteenth hole, preferably in gold.'"

Shadow rolled his eyes silently. Even in death the man sounded insufferable.

"Is that likely? How much was he worth?" he asked.

"Honestly, I don't know. I do know that he gave the impression of being hugely successful, but his apartment was rented, not owned. We dealt with the lease agreement."

"I don't suppose Francesca French was a client of yours as well?"

"Spencer Knight's partner in crime and heaven knows what else? No, she wasn't, but we represented Major Armitage during their divorce. Why?"

"She's dead as well."

"Good Lord! Murdered too?"

"Yes," sighed Shadow. "What can you tell me about the divorce? Was it acrimonious?"

"No, not at all. In fact, for a career soldier, the major seemed to have no fight in him whatsoever. 'Give her whatever she wants' was his response to her, if I may say so, rather greedy requests."

"She didn't leave him with much?"

"Wiped him out I'd say."

"And she was buying a cottage."

"So I understand, although we weren't involved in the purchase. However, I believe she was using the redundancy money she received when she left the bank to fund that particular purchase, not money from the divorce settlement."

"Thank you. That's very helpful. By the way, before you go, you don't play golf yourself, do you?"

"Certainly not. Whoever it was who said it spoils a good walk, I agree with them wholeheartedly."

When he'd finished the call, Shadow made his way down to the incident room and found Sophie there chatting to Jimmy.

"Hi, Chief. I thought I'd pop by and let you know what I've found so far. I guessed you wouldn't want to come to the morgue. Having examined the sabre again, I'm almost certain that's the weapon that killed her. The length, width and curve of the blade match the wound perfectly. As I said, a very professional job. One thrust managed to pierce the right kidney, liver, gall bladder and just nick the celiac artery."

Shadow held up his hand. He could feel the room beginning to swim.

"Sorry," she said, handing the report to her husband. "All the details are in there, but the other main points are: she died quickly and at around nine o'clock on Sunday night."

"That's very accurate. I thought the cold was going to make giving a time of death difficult."

"It would have done normally, but we have Ben and Ollie to thank."

"Really?" asked Shadow. He was always slightly sceptical of the forensics duo.

"Really," insisted Sophie with a smile. "When they were examining the victim's car, they found a receipt for the champagne we found on the grass, and also a sandwich wrapper. They had both been purchased from a petrol station at 8.42. The petrol station is only about fifteen minutes from the cottage, and she must have eaten the sandwich on the way. The contents of her stomach had barely begun to be digested."

Shadow sank into a chair feeling light-headed again.

Sophie winced. "Sorry, I'll leave the two of you in peace now."

With a last wave to her husband, she disappeared out of the door. Jimmy went over to the water dispenser in the corner and brought him a plastic cup of water over.

"Thanks. If we do turn out to be dealing with two killers then I have to say, I think I prefer the poisoner's modus operandi. Any more news?"

"I've been chasing Ben and Ollie. They apologised but said they hadn't been able to get into Spencer's or Francesca's phones yet or to examine the sabre as it's been with

Sophie."

"Oh well, I suppose I should be grateful to them for helping give us such an accurate time of death. According to Lottie, Spencer was with her until ten o'clock that night, so that would rule him out as the killer. But had he stood her up or was she planning on meeting someone else? What about you? Did you find any videos of the dinner?"

"No, sorry, Chief. Some of the officers attending have got social media accounts but they are all private. Finance have been able to get some decent information on Spencer Knight and Francesca French though. One of the computers had all Francesca's bank statements on it including for the accounts she shared with the major."

"And?"

"The poor guy has really lost out in the divorce. It looks like he handed over all their joint savings and most of the proceeds of the sale of a house they had shared out in Bishopthorpe, although it doesn't look like Francesca used that money to purchase the cottage."

"Cornelius Rutherford thought she used the redundancy payment she got when she left the bank. Can you check on that?"

"Will do."

"What about Spencer Knight?"

"Jane doesn't think they have located all the accounts he has in his name but say he's got at least half a million in current accounts, probably a lot more."

"Rutherford said he didn't own his apartment. Check if he had given notice to his landlord." He paused for a moment, thinking. "It's much easier to disappear if all your assets are liquid."

"Do you think that's what he was planning?"

"We know he had plenty of enemies. Perhaps he thought it was time to leave York – even the country maybe."

"But one of his enemies caught up with him first. If Francesca had just bought the cottage, it doesn't seem like she would be going anywhere."

"Maybe Spencer was thinking of taking someone else."

"Lottie? She said he was thinking of going to London with her. That would make sense."

"It would, but we are still only speculating. Did finance say anything else?"

"They hope to have a full report to you within twenty-four hours. Jane said that Spencer's passwords were fairly easy to guess and that he didn't take security very seriously. Maybe he was so used to scamming other people he didn't think someone could do the same to him."

"Did the Janes find any evidence that Spencer had been scamming people?" asked Shadow, who was guilty of using the same password for every account.

"Not exactly, but it sounds like he was always setting up then closing down companies, here and abroad. Jane said she couldn't find anything illegal in what he'd been doing, but morally it probably isn't that great especially if you are one of his creditors. She said they'll make sure there's a full list of everyone who might have lost out so we can compare it to our suspects."

Shadow nodded, remembering what Cornelius had also said. "Well, fortunately, we aren't the morality police but perhaps someone has taken on that role."

"You think it's about money not love then, Chief?"

"They are the two most common motives," replied Shadow, turning to look at the board where Francesca's photograph was now next to Spencer's.

"Any chance it could be both?"

"Possibly. Did you find out anything about the golf club the major was at on Sunday?"

"Yes, it's the North York club, just off the ring road. The major and Spencer are both members."

"Good. Let's pay them a visit tomorrow."

"Are you heading home now, Chief?"

"No, I'm going to get something to eat. I haven't had a thing since I was at the Shambles pie shop, and despite your wife's and our sabre-wielding killer's best efforts my appetite has returned."

"You might want to take this with you," said Jimmy, handing him a compact disc in a see-through cover.

"What is it?"

"The recording Tom made of the pantomime. I put it on a DVD so you could take a laptop home and watch it."

"Thanks a lot," he muttered, dropping the disc into his

pocket.

"You're welcome," replied his sergeant without a hint of irony.

Before leaving the station, Shadow returned to his office to collect a bag of laundry. His plan was to dine at one of his favourite Italian restaurants, but first he wanted to drop off his dirty shirts at Maggie's laundry and hopefully persuade her to join him. However, when he arrived there was no sign of her, only her two assistants who seemed to take great delight in telling him that their boss had decided to fly to Spain a day early. He left his shirts with them and walked back down Goodramgate wondering why Maggie hadn't told him she was going herself. He pushed open the door of Catania's and was immediately greeted by a shout of welcome from the owner.

"You are back, my friend! How good it is to see you."

Gino shook him warmly by the hand and led him to his favourite table in the window with a view of the Minster. A second later Maria, Gino's wife, came bustling over too.

"Did you have a wonderful time with Luca and his family? Have you brought photos?"

"I'm sorry, Maria, I didn't take a camera," he apologised.

"Camera! You don't need a camera. You can use your mobile phone. Never mind, I shall email Luca. I'm sure he took plenty of pictures of your visit."

"I didn't know you had his email?"

"Of course. These days it is so easy to keep in touch with

people. Even His Holiness is on Instagram to connect to the faithful."

She quickly crossed herself before disappearing into the kitchen. Shadow took a sip of his Chianti and frowned. Was he being overly sensitive or had Maria been making a point with those last two sentences? Like Rose, she was good friends with Maggie. He'd known both women for years and trusted their judgement implicitly. They were never wrong. Maybe he should have called Maggie when he was away and at least have wished her a Merry Christmas. As a steaming plate of cannelloni was placed in front of him, he decided to phone her as soon as he returned to *Florence* and attempt to make amends.

"Maggie, it's John."

"Good heavens, so you can use the that mobile of yours."

He decided to ignore this barb but at least it confirmed that he hadn't imagined she was cross with him.

"You left without saying goodbye."

"I was in a rush. As soon as I heard the pantomime had been cancelled, I decided to take an earlier flight out here. The little ones were disappointed, but my sister said she'd take them to the cinema instead, and I promised them I'd bring them a present when I come back."

"Is it nice out there?"

"Heaven – and not too busy either. Even at this time of year, it's warm enough to sit out on the balcony and sip a sangria."

"I thought you preferred a gin and tonic."

"Oh, you know, when in Spain... Anyway, enough of the pleasantries. Get on with it."

"What do you mean?" he asked, feeling affronted.

She sighed at the other end of the line. "I mean, I don't think you phoned just to see how I am. I think you want to pick my brains about Spencer Knight, who I'm guessing didn't die of natural causes."

"We found your name and number in his files," he admitted. "Can you tell me anything about him?"

"He approached me a while ago, full of charm. He'd heard, I don't know how, probably from flirting with the girls in the laundry, that I was thinking of moving to Spain."

"Since when?" asked Shadow. It was the first he'd heard about such an idea.

"Since Sam moved out here. Anyway, Spencer tried to convince me to invest in some timeshare scheme in Spain. What he didn't know was that Sam lived near to the proposed scheme. I told him about it, and he told me not to touch it with a bargepole. He said the land it was meant to be on was in danger of crumbling into the sea. I told Spencer I wasn't interested and would play it safe and keep my money in the bank. I never heard from him again. Having said that, I certainly heard plenty about him. There can't have been many women he didn't try it on with, single or otherwise, just so long as they had a bit of cash. I expect there will be more than a few cuckolded husbands who are pleased to see the back of him."

"You could say that. I'm practically tripping over suspects. Do you have any particular cuckolds in mind?"

"Far too many to mention and it's not only the men either. There are quite a few women who were less than happy when he finished things. Oh, and you could probably add Len to your list too."

"Len Horning? Why? He's not married, is he?"

Maggie laughed again. "No, not Len, but he's no fan of Spencer Knight. He thinks he cheated him out of his inheritance from his great-aunt. Oh, I can't remember her name, it was a flower I think, Lily maybe, no it was Iris. Great-Aunt Iris. She was Len's late mother's aunt and lived in London, but she didn't have children of her own and was a widow. Len was her only living relative, so as she was becoming frailer, she came to live in a nursing home up here to be closer to him. Now it turns out Great-Aunt Iris was very well off. Her late husband, I really can't remember his name, was a stockbroker or a bond trader or something and had made a fortune in the city. But when she died, there was barely any money left. It turned out Spencer had befriended her somehow and started giving her financial advice and she'd lost the lot. It must be three or four years ago now, but Len was furious at the time. I distinctly remember him standing at the bar in The Golden Slipper saying he'd like to wipe the smug smile of Spencer's face once and for all. I don't imagine he's the only one who's lost out financially to Spencer either."

"So I'm hearing."

"Oh dear, I suppose it doesn't make your job very easy," said Maggie with a laugh and Shadow wondered if it was only her first sangria.

"When are you coming back?"

"At the end of the month. Probably. I'll play it by ear."

"Well, I hope you enjoy the rest of your holiday."

"Thanks. Good luck with the case. *Adios*!"

And with that she was gone. Shadow could imagine her on a balcony overlooking the Med, her sunglasses on her head and a sangria in her hand. He put down his mobile, picked up his glass of wine and replayed his conversation with Maggie. As was so often the case when he spoke to her, he was left with more questions. Len Horning had made no mention of Spencer Knight being involved with his great-aunt, but was that simply because he viewed it as water under the bridge? Spencer had seemed very keen on Lottie, but according to Maggie, he was usually only interested in wealthy females. Could Lottie have inherited some money from her mother? It seemed unlikely, but could there be some life insurance perhaps? He took a sip of wine and leant back. Most importantly, was Maggie really considering moving to Spain?

Chapter Seven

Down 4 (6 letters)
Her fat pater

"Good news, Chief!" declared Jimmy as soon as Shadow entered the incident room the next morning.

"You've got rid of your neck brace."

"Yes. Sophie said she didn't think I needed it anymore, but that's not it."

"You've solved both murders, apprehended the killer who has given you a signed confession and we can all go home for the rest of the day."

Jimmy laughed. "No, but I think we might have worked out where the methadone came from. Sophie and I were talking about it over supper last night."

"And they say romance is dead," murmured Shadow as his sergeant carried on regardless.

"I was saying that some heroin addicts are given a daily dose of methadone from pharmacies and one of our suspects could have a history of drug abuse and been storing up their daily dose, but Sophie wasn't keen on that idea. She thought pharmacists made sure the dose was taken before the addict left. Anyway, then Sophie asked about Arthur the whippet. I'd already told her how cute he was and that he's recovering from an operation, and she wondered if he could have been given methadone as pain relief. If he was, then that means Lottie, Rohan, Stan and Major Armitage could all have access to it."

Shadow nodded thoughtfully. "Yes, although I only really see Stan and the major as having a motive. Rohan barely knew the victims, however, I am keeping an open mind about Lottie, despite her age."

"That reminds me," said Jimmy. "I tried contacting the Beresfords' GP to find out whether Ann was ever prescribed methadone, but she's on holiday until next week. But I did check, and Lottie hasn't got a driving licence."

"What's that got to do with anything?" asked Shadow, who was rummaging fruitlessly through his pockets for an antacid tablet. The indigestion that normally plagued him had disappeared during his holiday in Italy but had now returned with a vengeance.

"I thought we could rule her out of killing Francesca if she couldn't get out to the cottage."

"She could still be capable of driving," he snapped, his growing indigestion causing him to be even more irritable than usual, "and if she was considering committing murder, I hardly think being caught driving without a licence would stop her."

Jimmy continued reading from his notes, undeterred. "There's something else too, Chief. I found out who was arrested for vandalising Spencer's car – you know the story George told you about."

"And?"

"It was Christine Treadwell."

"Am I meant to know who that is?"

"She's the wife or I should say the estranged wife of Owen Treadwell, the vet Rohan is working for, and it was her catering business doing the regimental dinner on Saturday night – the Chrissie Major Armitage told us about. So, what do you think?"

Shadow gave a deep sigh as he abandoned his search and turned towards photographs of the victims, witnesses and suspects.

"I think we may need to find a bigger board. For now, let's focus on those we know had motive and opportunity. Susan Edmundson had access to the props, but as far as we know, not methadone, and although she may have disliked Francesca or been jealous of her, she had no reason to kill Spencer. If your theory is correct, Lottie could have accessed methadone, but unless we have missed something there is no reason for her to want Spencer dead, although she may have been jealous of Francesca. Whereas Len Horning and the West boys may have had a grudge against the two financial advisers, but I struggle to see how they got their hands on either the methadone or the sabre."

As he spoke, Jimmy had been busily rearranging and labelling the photographs.

"That still leaves us with Major Armitage, Stan Beresford, and now this Christine Treadwell person, who may all have motives and access to both the sabre and methadone," Shadow said.

"I've been thinking, Chief," began Jimmy, and Shadow managed to suppress a groan. His sergeant had never quite grasped the idea that some thoughts should remain in his head. "You remember how the dean disguised herself as her husband and they both had an acting background too? The theatre prop cupboard is full of costumes. A bloke could easily dress up as a girl or vice versa. That's what they do in pantomime after all."

Shadow merely grunted as he tried to concentrate on the board in front of him, hoping it might reveal something so far hidden. Jimmy clearly took this as encouragement.

"They do say poisoning is a woman's crime."

"They do. But maybe that's what the killer wants us to think."

"Or it's like I said at the cottage. We could be looking for two killers. Poisoning someone is pretty different to attacking them with a sabre. One is pretty remote, the other…well, it isn't remote at all. You would have to really hate someone to ram a sword through them like that. I don't think I could do it."

Shadow gave up. His train of thought was going nowhere

fast with all these interruptions. "It's possible, but then it also raises another question. If there are two killers, are they working together or alone?"

"If Spencer wasn't one of them, then it's got to be together surely, or it's too much of a coincidence, don't you think?"

"I think we should pay a visit to the vet's place and ask about the medication Arthur is on, but first I want to speak to Len Horning again. According to Maggie, Spencer Knight cheated him out of his inheritance, something he failed to mention when we spoke to him at the theatre."

Jimmy glanced at his watch as he pulled on his jacket and began winding his long striped scarf around his now-bare neck.

"He'll be at the radio station. *Horning in the Morning* finishes in half an hour."

"Right, we'll go there first, then the vet's, then the golf club."

"Shall I get one of the cars?"

"No, we'll walk."

"It's meant to drop below freezing and they are forecasting snow later," grumbled his sergeant as he pulled on a hat too.

"It won't hurt you," tutted Shadow. "Well, assuming you don't slip over again."

"How is she by the way?"

"Who?"

"Maggie."

"Oh fine, you know. Enjoying the sun, sea and sangria." He grimaced as they stepped out into St Helen's Square. His indigestion was getting worse. Fortunately, there was a chemist's shop on Lendal.

"Let's call in here. You can check Sophie's theory about drug addicts and methadone," he said, hurrying through the door. He purchased his preferred brand of tablets and unwrapped the packet while Jimmy spoke to Mr Patel, the pharmacist, who confirmed what Sophie had said. Any addicts who were prescribed methadone took their dose in liquid form in front of Mr Patel. He thought it highly unlikely anyone would be able to take their dose with them or store it in any way. As they were talking, Shadow took out the notebook he had used the day before and jotted down the names of all those involved in the case.

"Mr Patel, are you able to tell us if you have supplied any of these people with methadone?" he asked. The pharmacist took the notebook and ran his finger down the list. He paused briefly next to Stanley Beresford's name.

"No, I have not supplied a prescription to anyone on this list."

"But you recognised the name Beresford?"

"There was a Mrs Beresford who used to have a weekly prescription with us for various drugs. A nurse used to come and collect it, but not anymore. I am afraid I heard that the lady died."

Shadow nodded and the two detectives thanked him for his time.

"We didn't need to wait for the GP to return from holiday after all," said Shadow as they continued on their way.

"But if Stan did manage to keep some of his wife's medicine, what would be the reason? His wife died months before Lottie started seeing Spencer."

"I don't know, but it does mean that he is our first suspect that we know for definite had access to both methadone and the sabre."

Two minutes later, they were standing outside an unassuming grey building behind the Tesco Express on Gillygate.

"I've never been to a radio station before," said Jimmy as they walked through the automatic sliding door. "It's quite exciting."

"We'll hardly be interviewing him on air," replied Shadow.

"No, but still, it'll be interesting. We might get to see inside his studio."

However, as was often the case, Jimmy's optimism was misplaced. As soon as she saw their warrant cards, the young receptionist quickly ushered them down a corridor lined with photos of minor local celebrities with the radio station's presenters grinning maniacally. She showed them into Len's office and asked them to wait. Despite the shiny gold star on the door above his name, the office was little bigger than a broom cupboard. Thanks to the speaker in the top corner of the room they could hear Len signing off, followed by an annoying jingle, then three pips signalled it was time for the news. The lead story was the sudden death of a local man during a performance of *Snow White*, followed by a report that a road near Sutton on the Forest was still closed due to an ongoing police incident. After the weather forecast told them that more sleet and snow were on the way, the heavy bass of a rock song began blaring out.

"Can you turn that racket down?" asked Shadow, who rarely listened to music that had been recorded after 1959. Jimmy stood up to take a look at the speaker then shook his head.

"I don't think so. It looks like it's a centralised system. They probably have speakers all over the building. I quite like this one."

"I won't be able to hear myself think let alone conduct an interview," grumbled Shadow as his sergeant sat down again, and began tapping his foot in time to the music.

A few seconds later, Len Horning bustled into the office. Today, the radio presenter was dressed in an emerald-green suit with a lime roll-neck jumper. Shadow wondered if it was possible he was colour-blind.

"Hello, hello, hello," he said cheerily as he shook them both by the hand before squeezing himself into the chair behind his desk. "Apologies, gentlemen, I couldn't resist. Now what can I help you with?"

"When we spoke to you at the theatre, you told us that

you met Spencer Knight when he joined the Ebor Entertainers," began Shadow.

"That's right. He joined our little gang last year."

"What you failed to tell us was that he also knew your great-aunt. I understand that thanks to Mr Knight, you missed out inheriting a large sum of money."

Len's smile faded as he adjusted his spectacles. "That was ages ago. All water under the bridge."

"How did he meet your great-aunt?"

"I have no idea. She'd only been at the nursing home about a month. Then when I called in to see her one day, Spencer was leaving. Apparently, it wasn't the first time he'd visited her. I asked him about it, and he came up with some cock-and-bull story about how he'd been visiting a client and just happened to get chatting to Great-Aunt Iris. 'What a character she is! Such a lovely lady!' Of course poor Auntie and all the carers at the home fell for it. 'Such a nice man, always brings me my favourite sweets and flowers.'"

"But you were suspicious of him?"

"I asked around, and from what I'd heard, Spencer Knight never did anything unless there was something in it for him. And he shouldn't have been bringing her sweets. She was diabetic."

"Is that what killed her?" asked Jimmy.

Shadow's jaw tightened. It didn't matter how many times he complained, his sergeant seemed incapable of letting a witness speak without interrupting them.

"I'm saying she was diabetic, that's all." Len folded his arms defensively. "Spencer Knight didn't do her any favours."

"But your great-aunt left him her money."

"What money? There was barely anything left. She'd given most of it to him to invest. Almost three hundred grand disappeared! What she did have left, she'd asked to be split between me and him. Well, after funeral expenses that was the thick end of nothing."

"That must have made you very angry."

"I'll say it did," he agreed readily, then stopped. "Ooh, now hang on a minute. You don't think I killed Spencer, do you? Why would I do that?"

"Revenge for losing out on a large sum of money."

"Look, I might have wanted to strangle the smarmy, scheming sod back when it happened, but like I keep telling you it was years ago. What good would it do now? Him being dead doesn't get me my money back, does it?"

"Did Francesca French know your aunt?"

Len looked a little puzzled and shook his head. "No, I don't think so. Like I said it happened years ago, before she started working with Spencer. Besides, I can't see Francesca visiting an old folks' home even if there was money in it for her. She said she hated those sorts of places and that they always smelt of boiled cabbage. Not the most caring woman I've ever met, our Francesca. In fact, I'd go so far as to call her selfish. Look at the way she didn't turn up the other night without bothering to tell anyone. I thought she'd have shown her face by now though."

Shadow exchanged a look with Jimmy. He was surprised Len hadn't heard the news about Francesca yet. Even though her name hadn't been officially released, York was a small city and word travelled fast.

"Francesca is dead, believed murdered. Her body was discovered yesterday," he said bluntly.

"Blimey! Francesca's been killed too? By the same person? What's going on? Is someone targeting the Ebor Entertainers?" he asked, suddenly looking worried. "Hold on! Has this got anything to do with the 'incident'—" he made quote marks with his fingers as he said the word "—the newsroom was reporting at Sutton on the Forest?"

"She was found at the cottage she'd recently purchased. Can I ask where you were on Sunday night, Mr Horning?"

However, before Len could respond, Jimmy jumped in. "I can answer that, Chief. He was here on the radio. I was listening."

"That's right. I was covering for Erin. She's off with laryngitis, poor love," added Len.

"She does Saturday and Sundays, eight until ten. 'Evenings with Erin, eight 'til late,'" Jimmy enthusiastically sang the jingle, earning himself a scowl from Shadow and a huge smile from Len.

"I can see you are a fan, Sergeant. Is that all, gentlemen?"

"You might have told me he was on the radio on Sunday before we started interviewing him," complained Shadow as they left the radio station and began making their way back to the city centre through the predicted freezing rain that was now beginning to fall.

"Sorry, Chief. I got a bit carried away with him being a celebrity and everything and I thought we were only there because of Spencer. What would be his motive to kill Francesca if she wasn't involved with his great-aunt?"

"That's not the point. And I don't believe he hadn't already heard Francesca was dead. You know what's like around here. Word is bound to have got out."

"But there's no connection between him and the stolen sabre either. And how would he have got hold of the methadone?" argued Jimmy, who seemed intent on annoying him this morning.

"Get Tom to check and see if he has a record, and speaking of methadone, let's visit Arthur's vet."

At that moment, Jimmy's phone began to bleep. He checked the screen. "Susan Edmundson called the front desk and asked to speak to you. She sounded distressed apparently."

"Have you got her address?"

"Yes, she lives in Dringhouses."

"Let's go and pay her a visit first then."

"By car?" asked Jimmy hopefully as the rain turned to sleet. Shadow agreed with a reluctant nod.

When Susan Edmundson opened the door of her neat mews house, she looked surprised to see them; in fact she looked in shock. She had removed her combs and glasses and her grey hair hung around her face as she stood staring blankly at the two detectives. When it became clear she wasn't going to say anything, Shadow cleared his throat.

"Miss Edmundson, it's Chief Inspector Shadow and Sergeant Chang. You telephoned the station and asked to speak to us. May we come in?"

She stepped aside dumbly and the two detectives went inside.

"Shall we go through?" suggested Shadow as he gently placed a hand on her shoulder and guided her from the hallway into the sitting room. The room had net curtains at the window, a paisley-patterned carpet, old-fashioned but good quality furniture and framed needlework hanging on the walls. A large fluffy cat was dozing on the rug and opened one eye to assess who was intruding on his space. However, the most outstanding feature was the number of photographs of Spencer Knight. There were even more than at his own home. It was like a shrine. Lying on the coffee table was an open laptop, clearly an expensive model.

"It's all gone," said Susan Edmundson as she flopped down on to the sofa. Shadow and Jimmy sat down opposite her.

"What's gone?" asked Shadow.

"My money. My pension. It's gone," she said, shaking her head, then she gestured to the laptop. "It's Spencer's. That's why I called you. I found it my bag this morning. Someone must have put in there."

Shadow looked across at Jimmy. His sergeant had his electronic notebook in his hand, but he looked as confused as him.

"I'm sorry, Miss Edmundson. What do you mean your pension has gone?"

She finally looked at him. "I had a pension from my time working at the school and I had reached an age when I could start withdrawing some of it. Spencer advised me to withdraw as much as I could and invest it, along with some money I inherited from my late parents. There was a new fund he was setting up only for his most valued clients, but he said as he was so grateful for all my help and hard work, I could be one of the first to be included." She was smiling to herself at the memory, and Shadow felt a pang of sympathy, guessing what was to come. "He said at the very least I could expect a forty per cent return on the investment. He showed me the statements and charts only a few weeks ago, but when I logged on this morning it's all gone."

"And you only found the laptop this morning?"

"Yes. I have two handbags you see," she explained, pointing to two leather satchel-style bags lying on the floor next to the sofa she was sitting on. They were identical except one was black and the other dark brown. "I use the black one for work and the brown one for leisure. I took the brown one with me to the theatre on Saturday night, but when I came home that night, I was so upset I didn't open it again until this morning."

"May I ask how much money is missing?"

"Almost one hundred thousand pounds, Chief Inspector. It's all I had to live on in my old age. There's a little still left in my pension, but it won't be enough. I simply don't understand it. Spencer was so confident about the scheme. I can only think Francesca must have done something. I've tried calling her, but her phone is turned off. Have you spoken to her yet?"

Shadow cleared his throat again. "I'm sorry to tell you, Ms French is dead. We found her body yesterday."

This news seemed to wake Susan out of her stupor. "But she can't be dead. Who will be able to tell me where my money has gone now?" she demanded.

"When did you last see her?"

"Friday. Very briefly in the morning. She turned up at Spencer's apartment looking for him, but he'd already left. Then she dashed off again. She'd been to pick up the keys to her new cottage from the agent and was quite giddy. Like a silly teenager. Then we all saw her that evening for the dress rehearsal."

"Had she and Spencer argued or had a disagreement recently?"

"No. In fact, they had barely seen each other, much to Francesca's chagrin. Spencer had been spending any spare moment with Lottie. It was simply a passing infatuation, of course, but while he was distracted, I expect Francesca interfered with his investments somehow and that's why the money has disappeared. Now she's gone, it will no doubt turn up again."

She started smiling as if she found this explanation she'd come up with reassuring. Shadow saw no reason to shatter what he suspected was an illusion. Instead, he asked, "Have you any idea how the laptop came to be in your possession?"

"No. I thought it was lost. Spencer said he must have left it at the golf club on Sunday. He'd done some work there while he had lunch in the clubhouse, before going to see Lottie at her house. They were going to go through their lines while Stan was at the theatre painting some scenery. The two of them didn't get on."

"Mr Knight wasn't concerned the laptop was missing?"

"No, he said it would be safe at the golf club and that he wasn't planning on doing any work until after the pantomime. He wanted to concentrate on his performance."

"And the last time you took the brown bag out of the house was when you went to the theatre on Monday night?"

"Yes, that's right." She stood up. "But now I've had time to consider everything, I really don't think there is anything to worry about. It was quite a shock at first, but as I said, all probably due to Francesca's incompetence. In fact, I wouldn't be at all surprised to find out that Spencer has explained everything in his last will and testament. I am sorry to have wasted your time, Chief Inspector."

Both detectives were now on their feet too. She looked so relieved and happy, Shadow decided against telling her that Spencer hadn't mentioned her or anyone else in his will and the only beneficiary was his ego.

"Not at all, Miss Edmundson, but if you don't mind, we'll take the laptop with us for our experts to examine."

"Of course, of course, Chief Inspector," she agreed. Shadow motioned to Jimmy, who quickly closed the laptop and tucked it under his arm before she led them back to the front door.

"Wow. Talk about delusional!" whispered Jimmy as they walked down the path towards their car. "She's never going to see that money again, but she still thinks Spencer is the best thing since sliced bread."

"Did you think she was telling the truth about finding Spencer's laptop in her bag?" asked Shadow.

"She seemed genuinely shocked. Why did you think she was lying, Chief?"

"I thought it just turning up in her bag sounded a bit far-fetched. She could have taken it the morning after Spencer died. She was at his apartment when we got there. Perhaps she already had her suspicions that he and Francesca had conned her out of her money. It would give her a motive," he mused almost to himself as they climbed back into the car. "When we call in at the golf club, we should check to see if anyone remembers him being there on Sunday, or if he really did leave his laptop behind."

"It would have been easy for her to switch the bottles and poison Spencer, but I don't see how she could have got hold of the sabre, or the methadone for that matter. You don't think there could be any truth in her idea of Francesca taking the money, do you? That would have given Spencer a reason to kill her, then someone could have found out and killed him in revenge."

"I suppose it's possible. Get that laptop to the finance team and see what they can find."

As Jimmy was about to turn on the ignition, his phone bleeped again.

"What now?" asked Shadow impatiently.

"It's Angela. Kitty, the last of the dwarves, is back at school. She wondered if I wanted to interview her at lunchtime."

"I suppose you should, for what it's worth. Drop me off at the vet's on the way. I'll speak to Owen Treadwell and find out about the methadone on my own."

"Okay, Chief. You know if you struggle to take notes without me, you could always turn on the record button on your phone. Do you want me to show you how?"

"No, thank you," replied Shadow through gritted teeth. "I'm sure I'll manage. Now drive and go slowly. The roads are wet."

Town and County Vets was situated on Nunnery Lane. Jimmy pulled into the car park that was empty except for a very old and muddy Volvo. Shadow got out and made his way towards the tall thin red-brick building. He noted the sign above the door only listed Owen Treadwell as a veterinary surgeon practising there and that he'd gained his qualifications at Cambridge.

Inside, the waiting room was almost as empty as the car park. About half a dozen blue plastic chairs were positioned against two of the walls that had posters advertising pet food sellotaped to them. Sitting behind the reception desk was a woman with blonde tightly permed hair and an even tighter bright pink cardigan. She was engrossed in a copy of *Woman's Weekly* and didn't bother to look up when Shadow approached her desk.

"Hello, may I speak to Owen Treadwell, please?" he asked.

"He's not here," she replied, her eyes still fixed on the page she was reading.

"What about Rohan Kapoor? Is he here?"

"He's with a client."

"Perhaps you could help me then. My name is Chief Inspector Shadow and I wanted to know about some of the drugs you stock. Could you show me your storeroom?"

"No. You'll have to speak to Rohan. He won't be long.

Take a seat."

Shadow slipped his ignored warrant card back in his pocket and was about to do as she'd suggested when Rohan appeared from a door in the corner. He was escorting a small grey-haired lady who was holding aloft a birdcage with a budgie chirping loudly.

"Simply add the supplement to Joey's food and you should notice a difference in the next few days, Mrs Hinchcliffe," the young vet said, and he guided the lady towards the desk.

"See, I told you he wouldn't be long," said the receptionist, and finally put down her magazine.

Rohan gave him an apologetic smile as he stretched out his hand. "Hello, Chief Inspector. How can I help?"

"I was hoping I could ask you a few questions?"

"Certainly. Let's go through here."

Shadow followed Rohan into the consulting room, and he closed the door behind them.

"Sorry about Deidre. She's only been here a few days. The agency sent her."

"Where is your usual receptionist?" asked Shadow as he took in the cracked linoleum flooring and the piece of cardboard covering one of the small panes of glass in the window.

"She left a few months ago. Since then, we've relied on temps and Christine occasionally covers the desk."

"Would that be Christine Treadwell? Owen's wife."

"Yes. They are separated but still partners in the business."

"Do they have a good relationship?"

The young man looked uncomfortable. "As good as any couple who are getting divorced, I suppose. Is that what you wanted to ask me about?"

"No, I wanted to ask you about Arthur, the whippet. Has he ever been prescribed methadone to relieve his pain?"

"Yes, I administered it myself. Once when Francesca first hit him with her car and again at the Beresfords' house when he returned there after his operation."

"Francesca hit him with her car?" asked Shadow. This was the first he'd heard of it. Hadn't Stan mentioned something about a squirrel?

"Yes. It was an accident of course. A series of unfortunate events you might say. Arthur was doing what he loves best, chasing squirrels through the garden of the regiment's HQ, and ran behind Francesca's car just as she was reversing at speed in the car park. I believe she may have had an argument with the major. She was driving a little erratically I hear. I didn't see the incident myself, but Stan rushed down here with Arthur as soon as it happened. He was in a great deal of pain, poor thing, and Stan was very upset. He and Lottie dote on Arthur."

Shadow frowned. According to Rutherford, the divorce between the major and his wife was amicable, so why were they arguing?

"May I ask why you want to know about the methadone, Chief Inspector? Is that what was used to poison Spencer? If it was, I can assure you I didn't leave any methadone with the Beresfords. They have painkillers for him, but they are in tablet form and don't contain any methadone."

"I understand, but may I see where you store the medicines?"

"Certainly, it's just through here."

Rohan led him back into the reception area where Deidre was once again engrossed in her magazine. There was another door next to her desk. Rohan opened it and Shadow noted he hadn't needed to unlock it first. The storeroom was lined with shelves. Over half of them were empty but the rest held various small white boxes of tablets and bottles. Rohan pointed to a tatty-looking leather-bound book sitting on one of the shelves.

"We call that the medicine book. Whenever we take something out of here, we are meant to note in down in there, so we can keep track of what's gone out."

Shadow didn't think this sounded like a particularly efficient or secure way to store potentially lethal substances.

"I'd like to have one of my officers come down and make an inventory, then check it against the medicine book, but I'll need Mr Treadwell's permission. Do you know where I can find him?"

"He's probably at the golf club. Christine will be there too, I expect," explained Rohan with another apologetic smile. "If you don't mind, Chief Inspector, I should really go and enter the details of my last consultation on to the computer. For billing purposes, you understand."

"Certainly. Thank you for your help."

Despite Shadow's aversion to cars and driving in general, even he had to admit he couldn't walk all the way to the golf club. He paced up and down the empty waiting room while he tried calling Jimmy but each time it went straight to voicemail. He checked his watch. For crying out loud, how long did it take him to take a statement from a little girl? Knowing Jimmy, he'd have probably volunteered to read the class a story or give them a talk on the joys of policing. Shadow was still frowning to himself when Rohan reappeared with his bag in one hand and his coat over his arm.

"I can give you a lift to the golf club, if you want," he offered. "I'm on my way to make a call to a farm out at Escrick."

"Thank you. That's very kind," replied Shadow.

Rohan put his bag down and quickly wrote a phone number down on a Post-it note.

"Deidre, this is my mobile in case you need to contact me," he said, but the receptionist's attention was firmly focused on reading her horoscope. Rohan gave a shrug, pulled on the long raincoat and collected his bag.

"Don't you need your laptop too?" asked Shadow, noticing the piece of equipment sitting on the edge of the reception desk.

Rohan shook his head. "Oh that's not mine, it's Owen's. He's always leaving it lying around. Mine was stolen when I was studying up in Edinburgh. Unfortunately, I haven't been able to afford to replace it yet."

As they drove along in the slightly smelly, muddy and grubby car, Rohan chatted away about how he had been inspired to become a vet after reading the James Herriot books, which was also the reason why he'd chosen to study in the UK.

Shadow nodded along. It didn't really surprise him that this young man enjoyed stories written long before he was born. There was an old-fashioned air about him and the way he expressed himself. Maggie would have called him an old soul. He wondered if he was disappointed by the country he'd discovered when he arrived here, so different to the Britain of the 1930s. As his driver chatted away, Shadow's mind wandered to his earlier conversation with Susan Edmundson.

"When you visited Arthur at the Beresfords' on Sunday, was Spencer Knight there?" he asked after listening politely to Rohan's account of a recent trip to the moors.

"Yes, he arrived about five minutes after Stan had left to go and finish painting some scenery at the theatre. I may be wrong, but I got the impression he had been waiting until the coast was clear."

Shadow nodded. "He didn't happen to mention losing his laptop, did he?"

"Not to me, but we barely spoke. I left as soon as I could. I didn't want to be a lemon."

"Gooseberry," corrected Shadow. "So you didn't hear him make any phone calls?"

"No, but he did make a big deal about turning his phone off. He said he wanted to give Lottie his undivided attention. They were meant to be rehearsing their lines."

A few minutes later, they arrived at the golf club, a single-storey white building with rather ostentatious pillars at the entrance. Shadow thanked Rohan for the lift and dashed inside as the sleet continued to fall.

Unsurprisingly, thanks to the miserable weather, the golf club member bar was almost empty. Shadow approached the young man wearing a bow tie and waistcoat who was polishing some wine glasses behind the bar. Discreetly he showed him his warrant card and quietly asked if Owen Treadwell was there. The young man nodded towards a figure sitting in the corner, close to the open fire. Owen Treadwell looked to be in his late forties. He was a large man with dark unkempt curly hair and several days' worth of beard growth. He was dressed in a pair of well-worn cords and a thick navy polo-neck sweater and was nursing a large glass of what looked like whisky. Even from where Shadow was standing, he could see a thick layers of black dirt beneath his fingernails. On the whole, he gave the impression of a man who had given up on taking care of himself.

"We do usually ask that members' attire is smart casual,"

whispered the barman as if reading his mind. "Owen always used to be so well turned out and one of the club's best players." He waved a hand towards a photo behind the bar. It showed a clean-shaven, smiling Owen Treadwell holding a trophy. He looked about ten years younger, but according to the inscription it was only taken a couple of years ago. "It's sad really," continued the barman. "You can't help feeling sorry for him. You aren't going to arrest him, are you?"

"I don't think so," replied Shadow.

The barman clutched his chest theatrically. "Thank goodness for that. The management aren't keen on any sort of scandal."

"Then I'll try my best to avoid creating any. Can I have a half of Theakston's and whatever he's drinking?"

Carrying both glasses, he approached Treadwell, who looked him up and down suspiciously.

"Police?" he grunted.

"That's right. May I sit down?" asked Shadow, placing the drinks on the table.

"I suppose so." Owen drained the glass he was holding and half laughed. "At least you're not the tax man. I doubt he'd be buying me a drink." Owen spoke with a soft Welsh accent.

"You're in debt to HMRC?" asked Shadow as he sat down.

"I'm in debt to everyone. Haven't you heard? What are you here for? Is someone saying I killed their gerbil? Being sued for malpractice is exactly what I need right now."

"I'm here about the death of Spencer Knight."

Owen smiled, showing teeth that hadn't seen a toothbrush recently, and raised his second drink in a toast.

"That was the first bit of good news I've heard all year. Cheers."

"I take it he wasn't a friend of yours?"

"I thought he was once. We used to play golf together, me and Chrissie, him and Francesca, but like they say, with friends like him who needs enemies?" He took another drink. "I hated the man. He was a liar and a cheat and I wish I'd never clapped eyes on him. He got us to invest in this pet insurance scheme. We remortgaged the house, the business, and he even encouraged us to get our clients to sign up to the scheme too. Then when it all collapsed, he washed his hands of us. Didn't care that we'd lost everything including our good name."

"I understand he also had a relationship with your wife."

Owen's bloodshot eyes flashed angrily. "He used her to get to me, or rather my money," he said, his quiet voice growing louder. "Chrissie told me about the pet insurance scheme like it was all her idea. He put her up to it. Not that she could ever see it. We were doing fine until he came along. Now if I'd known he'd talked Chrissie into this when he was…" his voice was growing louder and there was a deliberate cough from the young barman and Owen stopped himself "…he was sleeping with her, I might not have been so keen to sign up." He took another drink. "The bastard broke her heart," he said almost to himself.

"What about Francesca French? Was she involved in this failed business venture too?"

"Probably, she seemed to be involved in everything Knight did. She was another one who thought the sun shone out of his arse."

"Can you tell me where you were on Sunday night and Monday evening?"

Owen shrugged.

"Here probably or at the flat above the surgery. I don't remember."

"I'd like one of my officers to visit your practice and make an inventory of the medicines you store there. Do you have any objections?"

"Please yourself."

From the corner of his eye, Shadow saw Jimmy arriving in the bar and nodded a greeting towards him. He rose to his feet and picked up his half-finished drink. He didn't think he was going to get anything more out of Mr Treadwell.

"Thank you for your time," he said, but Owen had returned to staring at his glass and didn't bother to reply. Shadow returned to the bar to find Jimmy chatting to the barman about the state of the weather.

"You took your time," he complained.

"Sorry, Chief. Angela said Kitty is quite sensitive, so I didn't want to rush her."

"And did the sensitive little girl have much to say?"

"Yes, she was quite chatty, but I don't think there was anything to help us. It was mainly about how she suffered really badly with stage fright and that she'd like a pony for her birthday. Would you like to read it?" he asked, holding out his electronic notebook.

Shadow held up his hand. "Later." He turned his attention to the barman. "Was Owen here on Sunday and Monday evening?"

The barman frowned. "He was definitely here on Sunday, but I don't know about Monday. It's my day off, so I went to see the Ebor Entertainers' pantomime."

"Hey, so did we," said Jimmy.

"I'd really been looking forward to it but wasn't it dreadful what happened to poor Spencer! Oh, is that why you're here?" he asked, lowering his voice.

Shadow stepped in before Jimmy could answer. "Do you know if Spencer Knight left his laptop here on Sunday afternoon?"

"He was definitely here on Sunday. He had lunch, and I remember seeing him working on his laptop, but I didn't find it after he'd gone. Maybe someone else did. Like I said, I'm not here all the time."

"I understand Christine Treadwell works here too."

"That's right. She's the main reason everyone puts up with Owen. She's an amazing cook. Oh, but don't call her that; she prefers the term chef. She can be a bit prickly. She's through there in the kitchen," he said, pointing to two white swing doors at the other side of the room.

"Thanks," said Shadow, knocking back the rest of his drink. He motioned for Jimmy to follow him.

"Good luck!" the barman called after them.

Chapter Eight

Down 1 (4 letters)
Cash is my one vice

SHADOW PUSHED OPEN one of the doors into the kitchen at the exact moment a woman in chef's whites brought a meat cleaver down with a bang, deftly removing the head of what appeared to be a plucked pheasant. He flinched.

"Do you want me to do this on my own, Chief?" whispered Jimmy.

"No, no it's fine," insisted Shadow, taking a deep breath then wishing he hadn't as the smell of blood hit his nostrils. "Christine Treadwell?" he asked, raising his voice.

The woman looked up, her cleaver raised again. "Who's asking?"

"My name is Chief Inspector Shadow and this is Detective Sergeant Chang."

"You'll have to talk to me while I work. I can't waste any time. There's a function here tonight and I need to get this game casserole in the oven."

The cleaver struck again. Shadow tried to ignore the butchery and instead fixed his eyes on Christine's face. Her blonde hair was pulled sharply back and tied in a bun, making the skin of her thin face appear taut. Her lips were set into a determined line and beneath her grey eyes were dark shadows. Each movement she made was quick and sharp. Everything about her seemed wound up tightly and it felt like any minute she might snap.

"We wanted to talk to you about Spencer Knight. Is it true you had a relationship with him about two years ago?"

She stopped and stared at him. There was a hint of contempt in her eyes. "Spencer was the love of my life, Chief Inspector, even if I wasn't his. He was handsome, funny, charming and made me feel like a million dollars." She closed her eyes for a brief second, then opened them again. "When I was with him, I felt like a teenager again. Excited, dizzy, drunk on love. Those few months with him were the best of my life."

"What went wrong?"

Christine shrugged as she returned to her task. "It was my fault. There were always other women sniffing around him and a man like Spencer deserved my full attention, but I got distracted with work and everything else. I neglected him."

"You work here and cater for outside functions too?" asked Shadow.

"That's right. One of us needs to bring in some money." She nodded towards the square window in the door through which the hunched figure of Owen could be seen still clutching his drink.

"I understood you and Mr Treadwell were separated."

"If only it were that easy. We're partners in the vet business, which as I'm sure you know is up to its ears in debts. The only way out would be to declare myself bankrupt, then I'd lose the catering business too. So like it or not, Owen and I are stuck together, trying to get out of this mess on our own."

"Except for Rohan Kapoor."

Her lips twitched into a small smile. "Rohan's been a godsend. Owen couldn't even remember hiring him or when he was due to start and I'm sure we aren't paying him enough. He's been doing the work of two vets and all the out-of-hours calls. The poor kid lives in the flat above the surgery so he's had to put up with Owen too."

She switched her cleaver for a knife and set about skinning one of the birds. For the first time in his life, Shadow thought he might have to become a vegetarian.

"Where do you live now?" he asked.

"With my parents. We had to sell the house." She shook her head as she briskly deboned another bird. "If you want the definition of *humiliation*, it's moving back in with your mum and dad when you're thirty-nine."

"Your husband seems to think Mr Knight was the cause of your financial problems as well as the breakdown of your marriage."

Christine snorted. "That's typical of him, always blaming

someone else. If he'd followed Spencer's advice and invested what he suggested, we would have been fine. The insurance company would have been a success, but oh no, Owen thought he knew best and only invested two-thirds of what Spencer said. If he'd only listened to me. Well, who knows what might have happened. Maybe things might have worked out between me and Spencer but instead his head was turned by that slut from the bank. He would never have got involved with her if Owen had just paid up and the insurance business had worked out."

"Are you aware that Francesca French is also dead?"

Christine stopped abruptly. A lump of flesh in one hand, the knife in the other. "Francesca is dead too? How?"

"She was killed with the antique sabre that was used to open the champagne at the regimental dinner you catered for on Saturday night."

"So Ian finally snapped, did he? I can't say I blame him. That's what comes of a man marrying someone twenty years younger than him. Francesca made a total fool of him. Spencer wasn't the first. She'd been carrying on with any young lieutenant who caught her eye and always making jokes at Ian's expense. I used to hear her at regimental dinners and cringe. Ian put up with it all, then she goes and leaves him. And then to top it, I heard she'd taken him to the cleaners."

"We believe she was killed on Sunday night, but Major Armitage said he was here."

A look of disappointment crossed her face. "Oh, well, that's true. He was here drinking and boring everyone with his army stories. We had to call a taxi to take him home." She paused again. "Hold on, did Spencer know Francesca was dead?"

"We don't know. We found her body yesterday."

Christine threw up her empty hand in exasperation. "Why didn't you find her sooner? I could have gone to Spencer and consoled him. If he'd known, he might not have gone onstage and could still be alive now."

Her voice was becoming high and rasping. Shadow became aware that her whole body was shaking, including the hand holding the knife. His sergeant had noticed too.

"Why don't you put the knife down and I'll make you a cup of tea, Mrs Treadwell. Would you like me to get Mr Treadwell?" suggested Jimmy gently.

The sound of her husband's name seemed to bring Christine out of whatever state she was in. She gave Jimmy a scornful look. "What possible use would he be?" she snapped.

"Where were you on Sunday evening?" asked Shadow.

"We finished serving lunch here at about four. I cleared up then went home to my mum and dad's."

"And on Monday evening?"

"At the surgery trying to make sense of the accounts, and before you ask nobody else was there. Or at least nobody conscious." She gave another scathing look in the direction of her husband then reached for a large saucepan. "Now if that's all, I need to get on."

Shadow and Jimmy murmured their thanks before leaving the kitchen and walking back through the bar.

"Well, she seemed a bit unhinged. And what is it with all these women giving Spencer Knight the benefit of the doubt, no matter how badly he behaved?" asked Jimmy as soon as they stepped outside. "What do you think, Chief? Christine was certainly handy with a knife, and she was at the regimental dinner when the sabre was stolen, and she hated Francesca. I bet she could have easily skewered her."

"Can we avoid that expression please, Sergeant?" replied Shadow, who had been looking forward to his lunch before spending time in the golf club kitchen. "I agree she had a motive and possibly the opportunity to kill Francesca, and it's also possible she could have access to methadone, but why kill Spencer? It's obvious she still feels strongly about him."

"Like I said, Chief: she's unhinged."

Shadow frowned as he climbed into the car. "When you give the finance team Spencer's laptop, ask them if they can look at the company accounts for Town and County Vets, and I want Tom over there going through all the records for the store cupboard and checking the medicines are all accounted for. The place is a shambles. If I was a betting man, I'd say Sophie was right and the methadone came from there."

Jimmy got to work on his phone, giving Shadow a few moments of peace with his thoughts until his sergeant turned on the ignition. The North York Golf Club was just off the ring road. Christine and Owen Treadwell, Spencer Knight and Major Armitage had all been here on Sunday.

"How long do you think it would take to get from here to the cottage where we found Francesca?" he asked as they turned on to the long driveway that led down to the clubhouse.

"On a Sunday evening, I'd guess half an hour at the most."

Shadow nodded. They knew Major Armitage had spent most of Sunday at the club, as had Owen, and it sounded like neither was in a fit state to drive, but Christine's alibi was a bit flimsy. Spencer Knight had visited Lottie after leaving the club and spent the evening with her. It was frustrating, but what was really bothering him was why hadn't anyone at the golf club found Spencer's laptop?

WHEN THEY ARRIVED back at the station, they found Ben, Ollie and Sophie all waiting for them. The two scientists were looking particularly pleased with themselves.

"We found something on the sabre," announced Ben.

"A fingerprint?" asked Jimmy hopefully.

"No. A hair. Only a very small one, but it was caught in

this curved part of the handle."

He began tapping away at the computer on the desk in front of him and then turned the screen to show them close-up photos of the handle of the sabre and a hair that was about half an inch long.

"Our first thought was that it came from the back of a man's hand," Ollie explained, then glancing across to Sophie: "We weren't being non-inclusive or anything, we are aware that women do also have fine hairs on the backs of their hands, but in this case the hand would need to be larger than average to press against this particular part of the handle and—"

"That's fine, Ollie," interrupted Sophie. "I'm more than happy not to be included in the hairy hand brigade."

"Have you got a match for the hair?" asked Shadow impatiently.

"Yes, Chief. It's Spencer Knight's."

"So he killed Francesca?" asked Jimmy.

"Possibly, but actually, it's a bit more complicated," replied Ben as he put up more photos on the screen. "We've had these images enlarged. Now on this one you'll see the hair we found on the handle. Notice anything unusual?"

"The root or follicle is missing," said Sophie almost immediately.

"Exactly!" agreed Ollie. "We carried out a fairly basic experiment. I used a pair of tweezers with edges similar to the width of the joint in the handle where the hair was trapped and removed ten hairs from the back of Ben's hand."

Ben obligingly raised his left hand to show a series of small red dots.

"Ouch!" said Jimmy, sympathetically patting Ben on the shoulder.

"Did this torturing of your colleague lead to any conclusion?" enquired Shadow.

"Yes. We don't think the hair came from the back of the hand. Each time I extracted a hair the follicle came with it. Also, we'd need to check the victim's hand, but we think the hair was too long to come from there and instead came from his head and was trimmed down and placed in the handle."

"Tom told us the dressing rooms at the theatre were left unlocked. It would have been quite easy for someone to go into Spencer's and remove some hair from a brush or a comb, the floor even," added Ben.

"But why?" asked Shadow. "What would be the point of framing Spencer only to kill him anyway?"

"Maybe we are back to the theory of there being two killers," suggested Jimmy.

"Or maybe it's a classic red herring. Something to throw us off the scent and waste our time thinking about it," said Sophie, who tapped her watch and gave her husband a meaningful look. "Speaking of time, I've booked us a table at that new tapas place on Fossgate to celebrate no more cervical collar. You're all welcome to join us. I'm sure they'll be able to squeeze you in."

"No thanks, Soph," said Ben. "We really want to nip down to the morgue and take a look at Spencer Knight's hand. If you have no objection that is?"

"Be my guest," replied Sophie as the two scientists headed towards the door.

"Hold on," called out Shadow. "As fascinating as the discovery of this hair is, there is more to the investigation. What's happening with all that stuff Susan Edmundson was shredding? Have you managed to piece any of it together yet?"

Both the scientists looked shifty.

"We were a bit snowed under, so we asked Tom to see if he could have a try," said Ben.

"This isn't pass the parcel, gentlemen. What about Spencer's phone? Have you managed to open it?"

"Oh yes, didn't we tell you?"

"No, you failed to mention it," replied Shadow, who felt like he was clinging on to the last shreds of patience with his fingernails.

"Well, we didn't find much. It looked like Spencer was in the habit of deleting his messages, emails and records of any calls on a daily basis."

"Interestingly, the only messages he did keep were from Lottie Beresford. He seemed pretty loved up."

"Would you say she felt the same?"

Ben shrugged. "I'd say she seemed a bit cooler, but I'm not an expert on these things. We can get their conversations sent over if you'd like to take a look, Chief."

Shadow bit back a sarcastic retort and instead managed to say, "Yes, that would be helpful, Ben. We know Spencer was involved with a long list of women. Did you find any compromising photographs or had they been deleted too?"

"Are you thinking blackmail could be a motive?" asked Jimmy.

"We already have plenty to consider. It would be nice to rule something out," replied Shadow.

"Most photos were of him and Lottie and a few of Francesca. Nothing worth killing him over, Chief," replied Ollie.

"And Francesca's phone?"

Another guilty look was exchanged.

"Sorry, nothing yet. We got a bit distracted with finding the hair."

"All right, well, off you go then and see if your theory works out."

"We'll let you know what we find at the morgue," Ben called over his shoulder as the two of them rapidly retreated through the door.

"What about you, Chief?" asked Jimmy as he helped Sophie on with her coat. "Would you like to join us?"

"No thanks. I'm planning on going to Francesco and Lucia's place. I'm not sure Spanish food is really my thing."

"It wouldn't hurt to broaden your horizons occasionally, Chief. Paella isn't all that different to risotto," replied Sophie as Jimmy tried to shush her while he ushered her out the door.

"Don't wind him up. You know what he's like. He's not keen on change," Shadow could hear him whisper as they made their way down the corridor. He waited until they were gone, then sat on the edge of the nearest desk and removed his phone from his pocket. He counted ten rings before it was answered.

"Goodness I am honoured – two phone calls in one week."

"I wanted to pick your brains again."

"Yes, thanks, I'm fine and still having a fabulous time."

"I was going to ask you that after."

"Okay, off you go. What's so important?"

"You said before you didn't know how Spencer Knight found out you wanted to move to Spain."

"Yes, it was odd. I barely knew the man."

"Have you always banked at the Blackcliffe and Rose?"

"Yes, I have done since I was sixteen and got my first Saturday job. It was at that little café on High Petergate, which had walls papered in sheet music. They made the most wonderful French onion soup."

"Yes, yes, I remember. Now did you happen to go to the bank and discuss buying a place in Spain?"

"Yes, I did as it happens. I spoke to one of their advisers about getting a bridging loan, but apparently they don't do them anymore. She was quite off-hand. Told me they hadn't offered them for years."

"This adviser wasn't Francesca French, by any chance?"

"Yes, it was. How did you know?"

"She's been killed as well."

"Oh my goodness! By the same person who killed Spencer?"

"I'm not sure, but I have a theory that she was passing information to Spencer Knight long before she started working with him. I think she pointed him in the direction of wealthy single females."

"That doesn't sound like very ethical behaviour. Is it allowed?"

"It probably breaks some sort of client confidentiality agreement, not that it matters now."

"Oh dear. I can't say I liked the woman, but she didn't deserve that. You really have got your hands full. Now I must go, I'm meeting Sam and his girlfriend for dinner, and I'm already running late. Good luck with the case."

And with that she was gone.

It was still sleeting heavily when he left the station. He put his collar up and his head down and hurried to Petergate only to remember when he arrived at La Scuola Femminile and found it in darkness that Francesco and Lucia always closed for a few weeks at this time of year so they could visit family back in Italy. As a cold drop of rain trickled down his neck, he sincerely wished he was there with them. By now he was too cold and wet to face sitting in another restaurant, so he headed home. Resigned to the fact that he would have to eat on board *Florence*, he called in to the Sainsbury's on Ouse Bridge and grabbed a frozen pizza and bottle of wine. As he fumbled for his glasses and tried to work out how to use the self-service checkout, he realised he had picked up a Rioja rather than his usual Valpolicella. It would have to do. He couldn't face upsetting either the tutting queue of impatient students behind him or the assistant who was stacking shelves and had glared at him as his wet shoes had squelched across her newly mopped floor.

Back on *Florence*, he lit the little wood-burning stove, then changed into his dressing gown and poured himself a glass of the Spanish wine while he waited for the oven to heat up.

He put on his favourite Ella Fitzgerald album, but even her magnificent voice couldn't improve the taste or texture of the pizza. After throwing the majority of it in the bin, he absent-mindedly began dealing out an old deck of playing cards. He tried patience and clock patience without much success then switched to pairs, a game he hadn't played since Luisa was alive. As he turned over the cards two at a time, his mind drifted back to the case and Jimmy's comments about looking for two killers. It was true: all the suspects did seem to have natural allies or perhaps accomplices. There were the two Wests, although they seemed unlikely. Stanley and his daughter – Lottie – or Stanley and the major: his old commanding officer. Owen and his wife, Christine, who while they may not like each other certainly needed each other financially. Len and Malcolm, who were old friends, although Shadow was still struggling to see Malcolm being involved. That only left Susan Edmundson, who didn't seem to have any natural allies.

Deciding it wasn't much fun playing pairs alone, he drained his last glass of the Spanish wine and grudgingly had to admit that the Rioja had been more than acceptable and went to bed.

THE PREVIOUS NIGHT'S heavy rain had slowed to a mere drizzle when Shadow stepped on to the towpath the next morning. As he trudged along dodging puddles with his hands thrust deep into his pockets, he didn't hear anyone calling out to him at first. It was only when the scruffy spaniel, barking loudly, ran in front of him as he reached the steps of Skeldergate Bridge that he looked up.

"Are you going deaf in your old age?" asked Jake.

Shadow scowled. "I've got a lot on my mind. What do you want?"

"The Environment Agency have issued a flood warning for the Ouse. They said the level will peak at noon."

"So?"

"So, if it gets as high as they are saying, the river will burst its banks. What are you going to do about *Florence*?"

"I'll keep an eye on the river. As I said, I've a lot on."

He knew he sounded defensive, but he wasn't entirely happy about being lectured on what to do with his home by someone who had only borrowed her for a few weeks. Normally, when the river levels rose, he moved *Florence* down to Naburn marina, but that wasn't usually when he was in the middle of a double murder investigation.

"Give me the keys and I'll move her to the marina. You can get a taxi or one of your lackeys to run you out to Naburn later."

Shadow had to fight his urge to argue as he realised Jake was right. If the river did burst its banks, *Florence* could be badly damaged. She would be much safer with Jake. He handed his keys over, and without another word Jake turned back and walked towards *Florence*, Missy at his heels.

"And they're not lackeys. They are highly trained police officers," Shadow called out after him.

"Not the ones I've met and I've met them all," he shot back without bothering to turn around. Missy barked twice as if in agreement.

For the second morning in a row, Shadow managed to complete his breakfast and the *Yorkshire Post* crossword without any interruptions. However, before heading to the Guildhall, he decided to take a detour to the radio station. He wanted to check what Maggie had told him with Len. Passing by the supermarket, he noticed the local paper in the window.

Local Businesswoman Killed – Is there a double murderer on the loose? Police won't say.

MacNab clearly hadn't taken kindly to the lack of information from the media team. Shaking his head, Shadow continued on his way. He checked his watch as he entered the radio station. It was a few minutes after ten. The receptionist looked wary as Shadow approached her desk.

"Would it be possible to speak with Mr Horning?" he asked.

The young woman frowned. "Not really. He's working."

"I see," he replied, thinking he must have got the time Len finished his show wrong. "Please could you ask him to call Chief Inspector Shadow."

"Okay," she replied and returned to scrolling through her phone.

As he was about the leave, the pop song stopped playing and an excitable-sounding young woman began chattering away about how it wasn't too late to enter a competition.

"That isn't Len Horning speaking. You said he was on air."

"No, I said he was working. He's recording Erin's Sunday show. She still isn't well."

"The show that goes out on Sunday is recorded?"

"Not when Erin does it. But Len would be knackered on Monday morning if he'd been working late Sunday."

"So last Sunday's evening show was recorded too? It didn't go out live?"

She rolled her eyes. "I just said, didn't I?"

Shadow was about to demand that she contact Len immediately when at that moment the man himself appeared.

"Oh, hello there, Chief Inspector. I was—"

"On your way to record Sunday's show as you did last week," interrupted Shadow and before Len could respond. "Why did you lie to us?"

Len glanced nervously at the receptionist, who was listening with mouth wide open.

"It's a bit delicate. I'll explain in my office," he said quietly before shouting over his shoulder: "Away from flapping ears."

The receptionist stuck her studded tongue out as Len trotted down the corridor and Shadow followed. Before he'd even shut the door, Len began talking very quickly.

"You see, Chief Inspector, I wasn't here, but I spent the evening with a young friend of mine. Someone you've already met actually." Shadow considered the possibilities for a second.

"Rohan Kapoor?" he ventured without much conviction. Len chuckled.

"No, don't be daft. He's a sweet lad, but a bit gawky, and besides, he's not gay."

"Who then?" He really wasn't in the mood for a guessing game.

"Danny!"

Shadow shook his head. The name meant nothing to him.

"Danny," repeated Len. "You know Daniel from the golf club."

"You mean the barman?"

"That's right. We've been seeing each other for a while now."

"He came to see you in the pantomime on Monday."

Len beamed. "Yes, wasn't that sweet of him? We had planned to go out for dinner afterwards, but then Spencer went and died, so I texted him and told him to go home. I didn't want him getting involved."

"Why didn't you tell us you were with him on Sunday night? You are both consenting adults."

"Danny hasn't told his mum yet. She's a widow and keeps going on about him meeting a nice girl. Then, when your charmingly naïve sergeant thought I was on air, I decided to go along with it. I didn't think it would do any harm. I mean I know I didn't kill Francesca."

"So the two of you were together all Sunday evening?"

"Yes, I went up to the club at about half seven and sat in the bar until he finished his shift at eleven."

"Did you speak to anyone else while you were there?"

"Well, I got talked at by Ian Armitage. I don't know about serving queen and country, but the major could certainly bore for England. I tried to have a chat with Owen Treadwell, but he was too far gone. Chrissie was there too, stomping around with a face like thunder. I'm surprised she doesn't curdle the milk." He laughed at his own joke.

"You know the major and the Treadwells?" asked Shadow. This was a link he wasn't aware of.

"Yes. Back in the day, they were all members of the Ebor Entertainers too. Owen had a fairly limited range, but Chrissie and Ian both had quite a stage presence. Susan used to tread the boards too in those days. We used to put on two performances a year back then. A pantomime in winter and something a bit more grown up, like an Ayckbourn in the summer. Then it all turned sour. Francesca split up with Ian and well, I'm sure you're aware that the Treadwells have too many problems to be prancing around onstage these days."

"Did you see Spencer Knight at the golf club at all?"

"No, but Danny said he'd been there earlier."

"I see, well, thank you for your time." Shadow stood up to leave and was almost at the door when he remembered the reason he had come to see Len in the first place.

"Who did your great-aunt Iris bank with?" he asked.

IT WAS AS he had suspected. Great-Aunt Iris had been a Blackcliffe and Rose customer too. He was now fairly certain that while Francesca had worked there, she had passed information about wealthy single women on to Spencer. Rather like the killer's motive, it was difficult to know if she had risked her career for love or money. His conversation with Len had helped to confirm the alibis of Christine,

Owen and Major Armitage for the time of Francesca's death, but it had also led to yet more questions than answers.

When he finally arrived in the incident room, Jimmy was chatting to Sophie.

"Morning, Chief, we were wondering where you were. We thought you might have got washed away. The river's due to flood later," said his sergeant.

"So I hear," grunted Shadow. "Morning, Sophie. What brings you here?"

"I forgot to drop off my report on Spencer Knight last night," she explained, pointing to a folder on the desk she was perched on. "You know all the gory details, but I thought you might want to refer to it when you write your own report."

At that moment, Tom arrived looking as eager as a Jack Russell who had just heard the word *walkies*.

"Morning, Chief. Hi, Jimmy, Soph," he said, placing the pile of folders he had been carrying on the desk in front of Shadow.

"You were right, Chief. The methadone must have come from Town and County Vets. Their filing system and admin are a mess, but I did a stock check. All drugs are meant to be recorded when they are delivered and then signed out, but there is definitely a vial of methadone missing and a few other drugs haven't been accounted for. I asked Mr Treadwell about it and the poor bloke broke down in tears. I think he'd had a few. His hands were shaking and everything. But he hasn't got a record. I checked that as well."

"Although he has been investigated for malpractice," added Jimmy. "There was something about prescribing the wrong dose of painkillers to a racehorse. He was threatened with being struck off. Actually, I'm not sure that's the right expression, but you know what I mean. The horse was okay in the end, so no further action was taken."

"Who has access to the drugs cupboard?" asked Shadow.

"Owen and Rohan obviously, and Christine still has keys to the place, but it seems the cupboard isn't always locked so anyone who was visiting could have got in there, especially as the receptionists keep changing and don't really know the protocol. Lottie and Stanley have both been there recently with Arthur; I looked in the appointment book for the last week," explained Tom.

"What about Major Armitage? Did he ever go there with Arthur?"

"Not in the last week but I'll check again."

"Good. Unfortunately, it doesn't look like we are getting much closer to eliminating anyone for Spencer's death yet," grumbled Shadow. "Although, I have just spoken to Len and he confirmed the Treadwells' and the major's alibis for the night Francesca was killed."

Tom tentatively raised his hand. "Are you sure about Christine, Chief? Only she's got a record. I checked her too when I—"

"For damaging Spencer's car," interrupted Shadow. "We

already know about that."

"Yes and no, Chief," began Tom as Shadow scowled. "She was cautioned for criminal damage re Spencer's car. However, there was another incident between Christine and Francesca French only a few months ago. The two women came face to face in the York Vaults. It was one of their live music nights. Insults were exchanged and Christine struck Francesca forcibly with the palm of her hand and knocked out a tooth."

"Impressive," murmured Sophie.

"It was actually only a crown so easier to dislodge," Tom began to explain, then seeing Shadow's face hurried on. "However, Francesca wasn't as forgiving as Spencer. She really laid it on in her statement. She said she'd suffered mental trauma and had to take time off work for dental treatment. Christine was convicted of assault, got a three-month suspended sentence and was ordered to pay Francesca two hundred pounds."

"That wouldn't even cover half the dental work," said Sophie with a grin as she jumped down from the desk she had been perched on. "It looks like you're going to be busy, so I'll love you and leave you. See you later."

Then with a cheerful wave she disappeared out of the door.

"She's in a good mood," commented Shadow.

"It's our one-month anniversary and to celebrate she got tickets for another pantomime seeing as I only got to see half of the last one. There's a professional production coming to the Grand Opera House tonight. It sounds great!"

"Talk about being a glutton for punishment," replied Shadow. "But she's right about us being busy. Tom, go back through the appointment book at the vet's. Go back as far as you can and look out for any names connected to this case."

"Yes, Chief. I'm covering the front desk for the next hour, but I'll get on to it," the young constable replied before following Sophie out of the door. Shadow turned his attention back to the board of suspects, but his thoughts were immediately interrupted by Jimmy.

"How could Len corroborate the major's and the Treadwells' alibis? When did you see him?"

"This morning. He lied to us about being at the radio station on Sunday night by the way. The show was recorded. I went to see him before I came here and found out he's got a motive for wanting Francesca dead too. I think it was Francesca who told Spencer to visit his great-aunt. In fact, I think that's how Spencer got all his information about which women were worth approaching. Francesca's position at the Blackcliffe and Rose Bank must have made her invaluable to him."

"Oh, that's a coincidence."

"What is?"

"Ann Beresford worked there too. I wonder if they were friends – you know with their husbands being in the army together."

"I get the impression Francesca wasn't the type of woman to have many female friends," replied Shadow, but Jimmy was looking puzzled again.

"If Len wasn't at the radio station, where was he?"

"He was at the golf club with Danny, who he is in a relationship with."

"Danny who was working behind the bar?"

"That's right. The bar where Owen, Christine and the major were and where Spencer's laptop was supposed to have been stolen from."

"If they were all at the golf club, then that only leaves Stan, Lottie and Susan who could have killed Francesca. We only have Lottie's word for how long she was with Spencer. Unless it was Spencer who killed Francesca and we're now only looking for his killer."

"If that's the case, then I can't see how the major or the Treadwells got the methadone to the theatre without being seen, which leaves us with Lottie, Stan, Susan and Len." Shadow sighed. "Let's keep focused and try to be methodical. Find out Daniel's surname, check to see if he has a record and if he can confirm that Len was with him on Sunday."

"Will do. By the way, the Janes sent over a report. It's on the desk next to Sophie's. They accessed Spencer's laptop and confirmed that there was a company set up with both the Treadwells as directors that closed with substantial debts. There was also a section marked Iris Hollins – that's Len's great-aunt. It looks like he took close to two hundred and ninety thousand pounds from her, and they have added other elderly women whom he was not related to but who did include him in their will. None had close relatives to contest their decision. I'll get the Janes to check where they banked. They also traced the account Susan's money was paid into and it was emptied into Spencer's personal account about a month ago."

"What a thoroughly unpleasant man he was. No wonder we've got so many suspects. Any news from Ben and Ollie about Francesca's phone or the mysterious hair they were so excited about?"

"No, but they have sent over the transcripts of some of the WhatsApp conversations between Spencer and Lottie."

Shadow wasn't entirely sure what a WhatsApp conversation was, but he put on his reading glasses and peered at the printout Jimmy handed to him. The messages from Spencer were certainly gushing and adoring, whereas Lottie's seemed lighter and more teasing in tone.

"What are all these symbols?"

Jimmy looked at what he was pointing too. "Emojis, Chief. To show how you are feeling without using words."

Shadow squinted again at the rows of little red hearts and yellow faces blowing what he assumed were kisses.

"He was over forty years old, for crying out loud, not a teenager."

"But Lottie is. He was trying to, you know, speak her language."

"She isn't using any of these emoji things nearly as much. No hearts of any description. There's only a couple of – what is this meant to be, a thumbs up?"

Before Jimmy could reply, his phone began to ring. While Jimmy took the call, Shadow wandered over to the window and stared down at the swirling brown river below. "Never mind the river levels rising, I think we are in danger of drowning in suspects," he grumbled to himself.

Jimmy finished his phone call with an ominous: "Okay, we'll be right down." He turned to Shadow. "That was Tom. Lottie Beresford is down at the front desk. Speak of the devil, eh?"

Chapter Nine

Across 7 (6 letters)
Pete initially used this portable device to contact a pal

Lottie was standing by the desk looking close to tears. Rohan was beside her looking almost as anxious as he awkwardly patted her on the shoulder. Tom was also there, along with a young female officer who was trying to console Lottie too.

"It's about the methadone, Chief Inspector," Lottie blurted out as soon as she saw Shadow.

"Let's go and talk in one of the interview rooms," said Shadow gently. He led the way down the corridor, and they all crowded into the windowless room. Lottie shook her head at the offer of tea and took a moment to compose herself. Shadow didn't hurry her and watched as she took a deep breath and brushed her blonde hair away from her face.

"I knew Dad had kept some," she began, "those last few days, when different nurses and doctors seemed to be in and out of the house all the time, trying to stop Mum from being in pain. They were administering the drugs, and I saw Dad take a vial out of one of the nurses' bags. She'd been up all night with Mum and was so tired, I don't think she noticed. I didn't say anything. At first, I thought he might give it to Mum to, you know, help her on her way, but he didn't, and I was worried sick he would take it himself. I searched high and low and finally found it in his shed. His man cave, Mum used to call it. It's full of all his DIY stuff. It was hidden amongst his tins of paint."

"What did you do with it?"

"Poured it down the drain. I know I should probably have handed it in or disposed of it properly. I'm sorry. I just didn't want Dad to have it. I kept thinking if he got depressed when I went away to college…" She trailed off. She reached for a tissue from the box on the table and started dabbing at her eyes. "Then when you said about how Spencer was killed, I got to thinking. What if he'd taken more than one?" Her voice broke into a sob.

"I understand," replied Shadow sympathetically. He stood up. "Thank you, Lottie. Please stay here with…" He paused, realising he didn't know the female officer's name.

"Constable Riley," supplied Jimmy quickly.

"Constable Riley. And when you are ready, she'll take a formal statement."

Lottie nodded silently, and Shadow beckoned Jimmy to follow him out of the room. Rohan also joined them, telling Lottie he wouldn't be long.

"Chief Inspector, may I have a moment of your time, please?" he asked.

"Certainly."

"I apologise. I know I should have said something earlier, but I felt I was being disloyal. It is only now Lottie has told me about her fears for her father's state of mind."

"Yes," said Shadow again. He resisted the urge to add "get on with it" – the young man was clearly struggling to find the right words.

"I saw Stanley take the sabre on the night of the regimental dinner. He slid it under the pad at the bottom of the cage Arthur was travelling in. I didn't say anything. I thought it was a prank he was playing on the major. I admit I don't always understand some of the major and Stanley's jokes. I just laugh along…" He trailed off.

Shadow stared at him incredulously for a second. "You should have told us this when you knew Francesca had been killed," he finally replied, trying not to lose his temper. "You could be charged with perverting the course of justice."

The young man raised his hands defensively. "I know, I know, and I'm truly sorry, but I didn't want to get Stan into trouble. I really don't think he would hurt anyone. He's a decent chap."

"Thank you for telling me now. I'll need you to go with Tom and make a statement," he said, nodding to Jimmy, who went to fetch Tom and explain the situation.

"Of course," replied Rohan, then he lowered his voice. "Afterwards, would it be all right if I take Lottie out for something to eat? She said she has been so nervous about coming to talk to you, she skipped breakfast. I would hate her to faint, but if you still need to speak to us…"

"That's fine, you can both leave as soon as you have signed your statements," replied Shadow as Tom and Jimmy joined them.

"Wow, that was quite a turn-up," said Jimmy as they both watched the young vet trot off with Tom to another interview room. "Both of them seeing Stan take what killed Francesca and Spencer. What now?"

"Now we go and arrest Stanley Beresford."

"Straight away? You think he's the killer? You don't think we should check the nurses who were caring for Ann Beresford? Lottie could have been mistaken. It must have been an emotional time. I really can't see Stan killing Francesca. I don't know why, maybe it's gut instinct, but I just can't."

Shadow held up his hand. "Your instinct might be correct, but it isn't going to carry as much weight in court as two witnesses who have evidence linking Stanley to both murders. What if Lottie's fears are correct? What if he is planning on taking his own life and we didn't act?"

Jimmy frowned but nodded. "I'll get a car, Chief."

LESS THAN AN hour later, Stan was under arrest and sitting opposite Shadow and Jimmy. Next to him was a duty solicitor. The young man looked far more nervous than his client. If Shadow had to sum up Stan's expression, he would have said indifference edging towards boredom. He hadn't caused a fuss when they'd arrested him. His greatest concern was leaving a note for Lottie and filling Arthur's bowl with fresh water before he left.

"I understand your late wife was given methadone before she died," Shadow began.

"That's right. For the pain."

"We have a witness who says they saw you take some."

"That's right," he repeated.

"Where is it now?"

Stanley shrugged. "In my shed somewhere. I wasn't thinking straight when I took it. I hid it but I haven't seen it since."

Shadow nodded. They had left several uniformed officers at the Beresfords' searching for any more methadone, but so far they hadn't found any.

"But you are aware that methadone was used to poison Spencer Knight?"

"Yes, and I'd like to shake the hand of whoever put it in that bottle, but it wasn't me."

"May I ask why you disliked him so much? I've seen some of the messages he sent to Lottie. He seemed genuinely fond of her and interested in helping with her career."

Stan snorted. "I'm sure all the other women he was involved with thought he was genuine too, right up to the point he dumped them for the next one. He did it to everyone, even Francesca."

"Are you aware that Francesca French has also been killed?"

"Yes, and I can't say I'm sorry about her either. She and Spencer deserved each other. They were both rotten to the core. They wrecked the lives of anyone they came into contact with."

"I understand Francesca and your wife worked together at the Blackcliffe and Rose Bank."

"That's right. Ann worked at the bank for nearly thirteen years. She started there when Lottie started school. Only part-time, but she enjoyed it, and it kept her busy when I was away."

"Were she and Francesca friends?"

"Annie thought they were. She was friends with everyone." He paused. "She'd always been worried about getting breast cancer. It's what killed her own mum. If the worst happened, she wanted to know she could afford the best treatment. She went to see Francesca after she'd left the bank and gone into business with Knight to ask her advice on taking out a private healthcare insurance. She thought she could trust her."

"And couldn't she?"

Stan snorted again. The hand that had been resting on the table clenched into a fist.

"The policy wasn't worth the paper it was written on,

but it did earn Francesca a big fat commission. There was something in the small print about not disclosing family history, but Annie had told her everything. That money, the money Annie was due, could have paid for her to be seen privately, get treated quicker. And there should have been something at the end, after she'd gone, something for Lottie. Set her up in London, help pay for her tuition."

Shadow nodded. That at least answered the question about whether Lottie had any money Spencer might be interested in. Despite Stanley being convinced otherwise, perhaps those messages were genuine and Spencer Knight, the ladies' man, had finally fallen in love.

"Can you tell us about Ann? What was she like?"

Jimmy gave him a questioning look. It was unlike him to ask about anything that wasn't directly linked to the charges the suspect was facing. But Stanley's grim expression had changed and there was the faint outline of a smile on his lips.

"I met her on the first day of primary school. The teacher sat us next to each other. It was done alphabetically: boy, girl. She was Ann Barrett then. She used to let me copy her timetables and spellings. When Derek Beardly joined our class the next year, I could have knocked his block off."

Shadow thought it sounded like him and Maggie, although it had always been Maggie doing the copying. She was always too busy enjoying herself to study. He often wondered what would have happened if he hadn't been sent away to boarding school. He might never have met Luisa. Would he and Maggie have got together instead? He realised that both his sergeant and the twitchy solicitor were staring at him. He quickly cleared his throat.

"You've always felt protective towards your wife and daughter?"

"What husband and father doesn't?" countered Stan. The grim expression had returned.

"So it would be natural to want to kill the woman who had wronged Ann and the man you thought was about to wrong Lottie."

"I didn't kill either of them."

"We have a witness who saw you take the sabre that killed Francesca."

Stan didn't flinch. "Then they are mistaken. I would never steal from the regiment, and I would never hurt a woman."

"Even one who had treated your wife badly?"

"Like I said before, I'm not sorry either of them are dead. They were a pair of common thieves," he said, echoing the words Major Armitage had used. "Spencer Knight stole everything he had, including Francesca, and as for her, what sort of a person cheats a friend and refuses to help her when she's dying? She and Spencer deserved each other, but he'd set his sights on Lottie. I did everything in my power to keep him away from her. Warned him, threatened him, even tried bribing him. If I'd known that sabre was at the theatre, I might well have shoved it through him."

"I'd like to stop the interview and confer with my client," the solicitor, who had been urgently waving his pen around, finally insisted. Shadow was about to agree, but Stanley kept talking.

"But I didn't know, and I would never have put it on the prop table where it might have been used against Rohan. Poor lad, it wouldn't have been fair. And while it's true I kept some of Ann's methadone, I was planning on using it on myself. After she'd gone, I didn't think I could live without her. I'd have used it too if it hadn't been for Lottie. I realised she needed me, especially with men like Spencer around. But I didn't put it in Spencer Knight's drink. I am very relieved that he's gone, but I didn't kill him."

As he spoke, his tone remained calm and he looked Shadow directly in the eye, unlike his solicitor, who had started to perspire.

"I must insist that the interview is stopped," he almost squeaked. "I would like to speak with my client and ask that he sees a doctor to assess his state of mind. He has just stated he considered taking his own life."

"Very well," agreed Shadow.

He and Jimmy rose to their feet, but he couldn't help hearing Stan mutter "That was months ago. I haven't lost my mind, you know" as they left the room. Jimmy turned his phone on as soon as they stepped out into the corridor and predictably it started bleeping straight away. Shadow left him to deal with it while he headed to the canteen. He normally avoided the place, but breakfast was a distant memory and his stomach had started to rumble. Unfortunately, the best they could offer to silence it was a milky cup of tea and a few custard creams.

Jimmy looked up from his computer when he walked back through the door of the incident room.

"Do you really think Stanley did it, Chief?"

"He has a motive, had opportunity and access to both the sabre and a supply of methadone."

"But he seems like such a straight-up sort of guy. The type of guy you'd have a pint with down the pub."

"You don't drink pints."

"You know what I mean. He seems really honest. He admitted hating Spencer and Francesca and keeping the methadone, and I believed him when he said he didn't take the sabre."

"Why would Rohan lie about it?"

"Maybe he was mistaken, like Stan said."

Shadow shook his head. "He described Stan taking it very precisely. The way he said he saw him sliding the sabre under the padding of the cage. He didn't sound confused or mistaken."

"I still think we've got the wrong man," replied Jimmy, looking unusually belligerent. "Tom said Major Armitage came to the front desk earlier when we were in the interview room. He insisted on making a statement – actually it was more like a character reference for Stan. Apparently, he was really brave in Afghanistan. Do you know he rescued two soldiers who had been injured? Carried them both to safety while under enemy fire. He got a medal for it."

Shadow sighed. "I'm not doubting the man's bravery or his service record, but look at it this way, perhaps he saw so many good people die in action, he had no problem getting rid of two rotten ones. Have you spoken to their GP yet? I'm struggling to believe that an experienced nurse, no matter how tired she was, wouldn't notice something as lethal as methadone had been taken from her bag, even if Stan has admitted doing so."

"The GP is still away and the nurses who visited Ann were from the local hospice. I'm waiting for someone from there to call me back, but apparently the nurse in charge of Ann's care has now emigrated to Australia."

"Of course she has," murmured Shadow as Jimmy continued updating him.

"I have got news about Susan Edmundson though, Chief. Her cat is epileptic."

Shadow raised an eyebrow. "Fluffy has my sympathy but why does that have any bearing on this investigation?"

"Actually, his name is Figaro, and it's important because his vet is Owen Treadwell. Tom checked Owen's appointments, and Figaro goes there for a check-up every week. He and Susan were there last Monday morning. Tom missed it at first because it had been listed under the cat's name. You saw how disorganised the place was. I reckon Susan could easily have sneaked in and stolen some methadone."

"What's her motive? She worshipped Spencer."

"But not Francesca, and I was thinking, what if Susan knew Spencer and Francesca had stolen her money and wanted revenge? Jane and Jane said the account she paid her money into had been emptied about a month ago. She could have been pretending she had just found out when she asked us to visit her."

"How did she get hold of the sabre? As far as we know she has no connection to the regimental dinner."

"I'm still working on that, but I think we should check her alibi for the night Francesca was killed."

Shadow gave his sergeant a wry smile. "You really didn't like her asking you to take your trainers off, did you?"

Before Jimmy could reply, his phone pinged.

"It's Ben. They've accessed Francesca's phone. It looks like she followed Spencer's example and deleted most messages and emails, but not the ones from Sunday. She tried phoning Spencer several times, but they checked, and his phone was turned off. It must have been when he was with Lottie. She sent texts that went unanswered too, pretty impatient ones by the sound of things. Finally, she must have tried emailing him, and this time he did respond and agreed to meet her at the cottage that night. Then the next morning, he tried phoning her, but obviously it went unanswered." Jimmy looked up. "That doesn't make sense. If Spencer did go to the cottage, then it seems likely he was the one who killed her, but then why phone her? Covering his tracks, do you think?"

"What time did he send the email?" asked Shadow.

"Seven thirty-two, Chief. Wasn't he meant to be with Lottie then?"

Before Shadow could reply, a strange noise started coming from his coat pocket. After a second, he realised it was his phone. He retrieved it and squinted at the screen. Hardly anyone ever called him. Most people knew he wouldn't answer. Seeing his sergeant's surprised expression, he said, "It's Rutherford," before answering with a gruff "Yes?"

"Thank heavens you answered, Shadow. Something rather odd has happened," began Cornelius, sounding unusually agitated.

"What's wrong?"

"I began proceedings to settle Spencer Knight's estate and, well, it's gone."

"What's gone?" asked Shadow, beginning to wonder if the solicitor had been on the Scotch.

"All of it. His cash. The bank accounts both personal and business wiped out. Although the majority of it was in the business."

"Have you spoken to the bank? What did they say?"

"They wouldn't tell me anything as I'm not the account holder. I tried to explain about being the executor, but it was like talking to a particularly dense brick wall. It was there this morning, but when I looked again this afternoon, nothing."

"How much was in the account?"

The solicitor hesitated. "Over a million and a half."

"What?" repeated Shadow incredulously.

"One million five hundred and five thousand pounds to be exact."

"Can they tell you where the money has gone?"

"No. It was one of those damn call centres. They said I would need to go the bank in person tomorrow and speak to someone, but I thought you should know."

"What's happened?" asked Jimmy as soon as Shadow had thanked Cornelius and hung up.

"Someone has emptied Spencer's bank accounts of over one and a half million pounds."

Jimmy leant back in his chair and gave a long, low whistle. "Wow! It looks like money might have been the motive after all. Doesn't Cornelius know who withdrew it or where it's gone?"

Shadow shook his head. "No, he has to go and speak to someone at the bank tomorrow, but whoever did it knew how to get through all the security procedures. Contact the two Janes and see what they can find out."

He began pacing up and down while Jimmy left messages for first one Jane, then the other.

"Well, I can't see Stan as some kind of financial mastermind. Maybe he isn't the killer after all," said Jimmy when he'd finished his call. Shadow scowled but didn't reply. Instead, he went to stand in front of the board holding the photos, questions running through his head.

"I bet Susan Edmundson had access to Spencer's account numbers and passwords. Do you want me to ask her to come to the station?"

Shadow shook his head again. He wanted time to think. Time alone.

"No, let's wait for Rutherford or one of the Janes to confirm the money is definitely missing. You get off. You and Sophie have plans this evening. Let's see what Cornelius finds out in the morning."

Jimmy reached for his coat and scarf and was almost out the door when he glanced back over his shoulder. "You know we could probably get another ticket if you wanted to join us, Chief."

"If that's your attempt at humour, I'm not amused, Sergeant," replied Shadow without taking his eyes of the photos of the suspect and witnesses pinned to the board opposite him.

After Jimmy had left, Shadow considered following him out to get something to eat, but the loud battering of hailstones against the window dissuaded him. Instead, he reluctantly returned to the canteen and bought the stale-looking cheese and tomato sandwich he'd rejected earlier. Before returning upstairs he visited the custody suite, but the doctor still hadn't arrived to assess Stanley.

Shadow took a moment to peer through the hatch in the cell door. Stanley was sitting on the bunk staring at the wall opposite him. His hands were resting on his knees and his face was expressionless. It occurred to Shadow that sitting in a police cell facing the prospect of being charged with two murders was not the worst thing that had ever happened to Stanley Beresford. He stepped away from the door and slowly made his way back to the incident room.

Everyone else had gone home for the evening. He sank into one of the desk chairs and tore open the plastic packaging of the sandwich. He only managed a few bites before discarding the rest into the nearest bin. Then he leant back in the chair and studied the rogues' gallery of witnesses, suspects and victims. Despite what he'd said to his sergeant, he didn't truly believe that Stanley Beresford was their killer either. He knew he was missing something, but he didn't know what.

The faces staring back at him gave nothing away. He couldn't shake the feeling that he'd been duped. Perhaps it was because he'd first encountered most of them when they were onstage, pretending to be someone else, but he felt that someone was still acting. Could Susan Edmundson have worked for Spencer and Francesca and really have been so blinded by her devotion to not realise what they were up to? Was she playing the part of frustrated spinster, complete with cat, a little too well? Everyone kept insisting that Major Armitage was the perfect officer and gentleman, especially when it came to Francesca. Was he just pretending? What about the Treadwells? Both of them appeared to be unstable in their own way. Had they been putting on an act while they hatched a plan to get their money back? Then there was Len, who had been performing for years, and Lottie, the best actress of them all.

Another barrage of hailstones hit the window, interrupting his train of thought. He sighed. Now there was the problem of Spencer's money going missing to further complicate things. This whole business had started with the theft of the sabre and now the victim's money had been stolen. If the money truly could be called Spencer's. He and Francesca appeared to have used every underhand tactic in the book to boost their own bank balances. He looked up at their grinning faces and remembered the photos in Spencer's apartment showing them in various exotic locations together. All those holidays paid for by other people's money. Shadow couldn't remember a time when he'd had less sympathy for two murder victims.

He picked up the bulging folder the two Janes had sent over and began flicking through. They had been as diligent as ever. All the companies Spencer and Francesca had set up then dissolved were neatly listed with accompanying dates. There were also lists of all the people they owed money to and those who had invested with them. Cornelius had been right. They hadn't only operated in this country. There were addresses in Spain, Portugal, Cyprus and Goa. The amounts were dizzying. He spotted the Treadwells' names and Iris Hollins. In the finance team's typically understated style, there was a footnote saying that they believed several of those creditors listed had since taken their own lives and so would not be available for interview.

Stuffed in behind their careful notes was what appeared to be the one and only piece from the shredder Tom had managed to reconstruct. Shadow guessed it was the final document Susan had tried to get rid of before he'd stopped her. About an inch remained intact, and Tom seemed to have used an entire roll of Sellotape to stick it together again. It was a handwritten letter from Ann Beresford. She was begging Francesca to get in touch with the insurance company on her behalf. Shadow shook his head. It was heartbreaking to read the words of a woman who knew she was dying, reaching out for help from someone she thought was a friend. He tucked the letter away and closed the folder. If it turned out he and Jimmy were wrong, and Stanley was the killer, he would have his every sympathy.

Despite the late hour, he felt no desire to leave the station. He couldn't face getting a taxi out to Naburn marina. Spending the night there on *Florence*, surrounded by other boat owners, held no appeal. They would no doubt want to chat and share stories about dreadful weather and rising river levels, or worse still invite themselves on board. However, his back was beginning to ache sitting at the desk.

Collecting his jacket and tucking the finance folder and the one containing all the witness statements under his arm, he left the incident room and made his way through the empty corridors and up the steep flight of stairs to the top floor of the Guildhall. After first checking that nobody was in the records office next door, he opened the door of the well-being room, flicked on the light, kicked off his shoes and sank into one of the sofas. As he rummaged through his coat pockets for some indigestion tablets – the stale sandwich was having its revenge – he found the recording of the pantomime. So far, he'd managed to avoid watching it. With a sigh, he decided he couldn't avoid it any longer. Who knew, perhaps it would help him find the killer; nothing else seemed to be working. There was a television set in the corner of the room that had a built-in disc player. Reluctantly, he put in the disc and pressed play. Then he returned to the sofa, pulling one of the fleece blankets over his knees.

The pantomime was every bit as terrible as he'd remembered, but no matter how hard he tried, he couldn't see anything he'd missed the first time. Tom had left it recording during the interval, and for fifteen minutes all he could hear was what he assumed were the Dawsons chatting between themselves about their daughter, how good Lottie was and where they should go for supper after the performance. That at least corroborated their alibis he supposed, but he wished Tom had been filming from somewhere backstage. The recording ended when Angela appeared from the behind the curtains calling for help. He flicked off the television and, yawning, decided to rest his eyes and think for a few minutes, before reading through the witness statements.

⚭

He was rudely awoken by the sound of a police car siren returning to the station. Blinking, he looked at his watch. It was half past five. He cursed to himself. He'd been asleep for hours. He couldn't waste any more time. They'd need to either charge or release Stanley soon. Rubbing his eyes, he reached for his glasses and began reading through the witness statements again. Last in the pile were the ones from the children playing the seven dwarves. He had briefly read them all before except for Kitty's, the little girl Jimmy had interviewed separately. It was a quite a long statement for a ten-year-old girl, but then brevity was not his sergeant's strong point.

It began with details of Kitty's arrival at the theatre with her mother. Apparently, they arrived at the same time as Rohan, who was walking funny because a Shetland pony had trodden on his foot. Kitty would very much like a pony, but her brother had allergies. Shadow sighed to himself. No wonder Jimmy had been so long at the school. He read on. It seemed Kitty was very worried about her performance and was suffering from stage fright. This was made worse when she found out Angela, or Miss Chang as she called her, would be going onstage and so wouldn't have as much time to help her get ready. Kitty was particularly concerned about who would help her put her hair up so it would fit under the cap all the dwarves wore. It seemed Angela normally did this, but everyone else rallied round.

Kitty found Miss Edmundson was a bit rough and pulled her hair. She nearly started to cry, but then Lottie, who Kitty thought was very pretty, helped and she was much better at doing hair. Shadow ran a hand across his eyes and yawned as he continued to read. Kitty was still feeling a bit sick, so Rohan took her to the door that led out on to the fire escape so she could get some fresh air and be away from the others who were still getting ready and who were making fun of her.

Kitty wanted to hear more about the Shetland pony, but Rohan had to leave her on her own for a few minutes while he went to give his laptop to Miss Edmundson for safekeeping. He had told her he didn't trust the two people who shared his dressing room and who were inside Dobbin, the pantomime horse, not to play games on it. Kitty understood this as her brother often played on her iPad without permission if she left it lying around and so she tried counting snowflakes until Rohan came back.

Shadow paused. When Rohan had driven him to the golf club, he'd told him he didn't have a laptop. Even if he had Owen's with him, he wouldn't need to keep it from Matt and Steve West. They were sewn into their costume. So, whose laptop was he so keen to give to Susan Edmundson?

All the pieces of information swirling around his head

slowly started clicking into place. He put Kitty's statement down and began sifting through the other statements. Steven and Matthew West had almost been forgotten, but as he read through the notes he'd made after speaking to them, he found what he was looking for. They said the twenty-four-hour helpline Spencer had promised was actually a number for a foreign call centre. Weren't a lot of these centres based in India?

He reached for the folder from the finance team. He ran his finger down the list of companies Spencer and Francesca had been involved with. It was there on page seventeen, KCC of Margao. Below was a brief note on the business. Kapoor Central Communications had been established almost twenty years ago but had gone bankrupt about two years ago. The owner and main shareholder was one Raj Kapoor. Shadow let out a long slow breath. Finally, everything made sense.

He smiled to himself as he closed the folder. Now even the little girl's comment about Rohan walking funny made sense. A pony hadn't trodden on his foot, he was walking awkwardly because he was smuggling the sabre into the theatre under that ridiculously long coat he always wore.

He threw back the fleecy blanket and checked his watch again. It was nearly seven. He removed his phone from his jacket pocket, but the screen was blank. The battery had run out. Grumbling to himself, he looked around and spotted a landline phone. He picked up the receiver then realised he didn't know his sergeant's number. However, one of the buttons on the phone was helpfully marked "reception desk" and the constable on duty put him through to Jimmy's phone. Jimmy answered after only a couple of rings and sounded remarkably bright and alert.

"Morning, Chief. Are you okay?"

"Fine, did I wake you?"

"No, I'm out on a run. Why are you calling for the well-being room? You didn't spend the night at the station, did you? You could have stayed with us."

"How do you know where I am?"

"They told me when they put you through from reception."

Shadow silently cursed his mobile. His spending the night up here would be the talk of the station. "Never mind about that now. Where are you exactly?"

"On Micklegate."

"Good. Get yourself over to Town and County Vets. I'll send a car. Rohan Kapoor is our killer. If you find him, arrest him."

He hung up then called reception again and told them to send two uniformed officers to meet Jimmy at the Nunnery Lane practice. Then he went in search of somewhere he could plug his stupid phone into. Having splashed water on his face and chewed a couple of indigestion tablets to freshen his breath, he went down to the custody suite and told the sergeant in charge to draw up the paperwork so Stanley could be released.

He arrived back in his office to find his newly charged phone ringing. It was Jimmy.

"No sign of Rohan at the vet's, Chief. We had to break the door down into the flat above. It looks like he's scarpered. All his clothes have gone. There was no sign of Owen either. I did leave a message for him to call you with the receptionist who was just arriving, but she seemed a bit clueless."

"That sounds about right. All right, get back here as soon as you can."

Shadow put the phone down, and as Jimmy wasn't there, he asked Tom to put out a call to all airports that Rohan Kapoor was wanted for questioning in connection with two murders and to see if any local taxi firms had taken a booking for a Rohan Kapoor. Then he asked reception to put him through to Bishop Askham college. It seemed to take forever for someone to answer. Finally, a wary-sounding man picked up. Shadow introduced himself and asked to be put through to the veterinary medicine department.

"I can't do that. They're not there."

"Well, perhaps you can help me."

"I doubt it. You've come through to the porter's lodge. Everyone else must have gone to the graduation ceremony."

"Where is the ceremony taking place?"

"York Minster."

Shadow quickly thanked him and pulled on his coat. As

he headed out of the station, he first phoned George and then Jimmy. He arrived at the west doors of the Minster as the ceremony was beginning. George was waiting for him. Students in black gowns and mortar boards were filing in through huge west doors. They were throwing their arms around each other, taking photos and celebrating with their families.

"We'll never spot him in this lot," said George, shaking his head. "There are loads of them and they all look the same."

Shadow knew he was right. "Can you speak to whoever is charge and see if his name is on the list?" he asked.

George disappeared into the throng of students as a police car pulled up on Duncombe Place with a screech and Jimmy jumped out. He ran over still in his shorts and hoodie.

"Sorry, Chief. I haven't had time to change."

"Don't worry about it. You never know, you might need to chase after him if he's here."

His phone began to ring. It was Owen Treadwell finally returning his call.

"Is Rohan with you?" asked Shadow without much hope.

"No, why?" he replied, sounding half asleep.

"Is he graduating today?"

"Graduating?"

Shadow stuck his finger in his other ear to try to shut out the noise of the students and their families. He spoke slowly and deliberately in case Owen had already been drinking.

"Bishop Askham college are holding a graduation ceremony at the Minster today. Rohan said he was taking his master's in veterinary medicine there."

"I might be nursing the mother of all hangovers, but I haven't lost my mind, Chief Inspector. Bishop Askham don't offer a veterinary medicine master's course."

Shadow ended the call, mentally kicking himself for not checking the young man's story. Before he could pass this message on to Jimmy, Tom arrived out of breath and waving a thick white envelope.

"This just arrived for you at the station, Chief."

Shadow tore open the envelope, unfolded the neatly typed letter and began reading.

My dear Chief Inspector Shadow,

I hope this letter finds you well.

Firstly, I must ask for your forgiveness for wasting your valuable time and also the time and efforts of Sergeant Chang and the other excellent officers you work with.

Secondly, if Stanley Beresford is still in your custody, then I implore you to release him immediately. Mr Beresford is not guilty of killing anyone. I could not let such a kind and decent man go to jail for any crime against Spencer Knight. Stanley and Lottie have both suffered enough.

I, Rohan Kapoor, confess to the murder of both

Spencer Knight and Francesca French. I am sure you have already discovered this fact, but in order to resolve any doubts, please allow me to explain.

My sister, Rakhi, and I lost our parents when we were children. We were raised by my father's brother, Raj. He was single and had no children of his own, but instead had dedicated his life to building a successful business providing call-centre services to companies based in the UK. Our uncle was a kind and generous man who happily paid for my sister and me to attend university here in the UK and encouraged us to follow our dreams.

However, one day, our uncle had the misfortune of meeting Mr Spencer Knight. Spencer presented Uncle Raj with a business proposition.

Our uncle was not a fool and was not about to sign a contract and invest in the business of a man he didn't know. Spencer then introduced him to his partner, Francesca French, who assured our uncle that she represented a well-known UK bank and they were also backing Spencer's new venture.

The promised business never came. No more than a handful of calls came through to the new centre our uncle had set up and the new employees he had taken on were left twiddling their thumbs. After a few months, he had to start letting them go and kept trying to contact Spencer and Francesca, but they would never return his calls. When he finally contacted someone at the bank and was told Francesca no longer worked there, he realised he had been conned and would never get his money back.

He was in debt and struggled to try to pay back local businesses he had always had a good relationship with. He had not only lost the business he had worked so hard to build but also, and most importantly to him, his good name. As he could not live with the guilt and shame, he took his own life. He drank a small draught of morphine to dull the pain and then fell on his grandfather's regimental sword.

Rakhi and I were devastated. This sad event not only meant I lost my beloved uncle, but I was also unable to finish the last year of my studies and qualify to become a veterinary surgeon. My sister was also forced to give up her degree in computer science. The two of us decided Spencer Knight and Francesca French must not be allowed to go unpunished. We went to the authorities in India but were told nothing could be done to bring them to justice, and so we decided to take the matter into our own hands and that I should travel to York.

It soon became apparent, when I arrived in your city, that my uncle was not the only one to have suffered because of Spencer and Francesca's duplicity. Almost everyone I met had been made miserable by the actions of this reprehensible pair.

I watched them carefully, listened to what others said and soon realised they had not changed. Susan had trusted them with the money for her old age. Spencer and Francesca only spoke to Mr and Mrs Dawson briefly but swiftly turned the conversation to their pensions. While I believe Spencer was taken with Lottie's beauty, I also believe he saw her talent as something he could benefit from financially. Her father certainly felt the same.

Although I had always planned to kill the two of them, I was unsure of how I would "do the deed" until the major told me about the regimental sabre. It was so similar to the one my dear uncle used to end his life that I knew at once it would be my murder weapon for at least one of them, then the idea came to me that I could poison the other with a type of morphine. I like to think of it as poetic justice. I stole the sabre when I went to collect Arthur by hiding it in his cage, in the same way I described Stanley had stolen it.

"The best lies are always based on the truth," Shadow murmured as he continued to read.

The plan Rakhi and I had hatched required access to the bank accounts of Spencer and Francesca. Therefore, when Spencer visited Lottie at her home on Sunday and I was there checking on Arthur after his late night, I took the opportunity to steal his laptop. With my sister's assistance I was able to hack into his accounts and pass all the necessary information on to her.

While the laptop was in my possession, I saw the email from Francesca begging Spencer to meet her at the cottage she had just bought. It was the perfect opportunity. Knowing Spencer had turned his phone off when he was with Lottie, I replied on his behalf so she would stop trying to message him. I then went in his place. I parked a little way up the lane and waited for her to arrive. Anyone seeing my vehicle would think nothing of it. They would assume I was visiting one of the local farms.

Afterwards, I moved her body towards the hedge so she was hidden from view. I managed to take the sabre back to the theatre by hiding it beneath my coat. I did this in case Francesca was found before I had chance to kill Spencer. I needed an insurance policy. I knew the sabre would be easy to identify as the murder weapon, so I placed a hair I found in Spencer's dressing room in the handle to point the finger at him. That was also the reason for me placing it on the prop table for him to pick up. At the very least, I hoped to confuse you.

It was very simple to poison Spencer. I prepared the mixture at the dispensary using the same bottle and food colouring as Susan. When she was distracted looking after the children, I put the sabre on the prop table, the laptop in her bag and switched the bottles. I hid the original bottle in the fire bucket. I am providing you with these details I know you have not released as proof of my guilt and to show that I am not simply trying to get Stanley "off the hook" (I am sure that thought may have crossed your mind, Chief Inspector).

My original plan had been to leave a suicide note in Spencer's dressing room, after he collapsed onstage. In this note he would confess to the murder of Francesca. However, I had not anticipated your presence at the performance. You and Sergeant Chang visited Spencer's dressing room before I could plant the note.

As your investigation began to focus on the practice, I knew I needed to act quickly. When Lottie confided in me about the methadone, I persuaded her to come and speak to you. I thought you would arrest Stanley but added my story about him stealing the sabre to be sure. The hours you wasted questioning him would give me enough time to leave the country.

Rest assured that my sister and I only took enough money to enable us to complete our studies. The rest of Spencer and Francesca's ill-gotten gains will be used to try to make amends for some of their cruel and selfish actions.

Please accept my apologies once again, Chief Inspector.

Yours sincerely,
Rohan Kapoor

Chapter Ten

Across 9 (9 letters)
Eve can partly generate revenge

"Wow!" exclaimed Jimmy, who had been reading over his shoulder. "He thought of everything. Where do you think he is now?"

"Probably out of the country as he said. Tom has put a call out to the airports but I'm not optimistic. You'd better tell George to call off the search and, Tom, you go and tell the two officers in the car over there to get back to the station."

Shadow watched Jimmy and Tom hurry away, then he wearily trudged back to the station himself, torturing himself thinking of all the clues he'd missed and how he'd allowed Rohan to misdirect him. When he arrived at the station, he found Cornelius waiting for him, red in the face and sweating profusely despite the cold.

"Busy morning, Cornelius?" he asked as the solicitor began mopping his brow with a large spotted handkerchief.

"I don't know what it is and quite frankly I wish I'd never agreed to act for Spencer bloody Knight."

"What happened at the bank?"

"First, I had to jump through all sorts of hoops to convince them of who I was, then I had to explain to someone, who looked like they'd only left school yesterday, what had happened. Anyway, according to them all the transactions were made yesterday via online banking and whoever did it passed all the security procedures and the only reference they gave was 'to settle creditor's account', then they gave me a list of all the accounts the money had been paid into. Not the account details, you understand, only the names, but I thought hurrah! This should give Shadow a motive and lead him to the killer, but what do you make of this?"

He handed Shadow a handwritten list, the words slightly smudged with the perspiration from the solicitor's hand. Shadow began to read.

Mr S A Beresford £250,000

Mr Len Horning £250,000

Miss Susan J Edmundson £100,000

Town and County Vets £300,000

West Tours Ltd £5,000

Marquess of Granby £600,000

"These amounts roughly equate to what each party lost because of Spencer and French."

"Really?" replied Cornelius, who was still trying to catch his breath.

"Yes, but I don't see why he did it. What's the point? They are bound to have to pay it all back."

"Who are you talking about?"

"A young man called Rohan Kapoor. I have a signed confession from him for both murders."

"So, congratulations are in order."

"Hardly. He's left the country probably yesterday after making these payments." He frowned. "It seems a lot of hard work if the recipients have to return the cash."

"Actually, that's where it gets even stickier. You see the payments were scheduled. That is, they were set up on Sunday to go out today, and on Sunday Spencer was still alive."

"I know, but Rohan admits to taking the laptop," he said, thinking out loud. "Does that mean they all get to keep the money? What about paying inheritance tax?"

The solicitor held up his hands. "I'm really not sure, Shadow. In fact, I'm not sure of anything at the moment." Then he pointed to the list. "And what's the Marquess of Granby? A pub?"

"I believe it's our killer's idea of a joke," replied Shadow. "I remember him telling me his uncle was also a kind man. I imagine you will find that account may be traced to India. It's probably been closed already." He looked back at the list. "There's nothing here for Major Armitage."

"Actually, Francesca had failed to update her will, so everything she had goes to him," the solicitor explained as he fanned himself with his hand.

Shadow nodded. It seemed Rohan really had accounted for everything.

"And he'll be allowed to keep his inheritance?"

Cornelius threw his hands up in the air. "Who knows? I would say yes, probably. I am quite happy to declare my ignorance. I can honestly say in all my years of practising law, I have never encountered a situation quite like this."

Shadow nodded sympathetically as Jimmy and Tom entered the station together.

"Ah, there you are, Tom. Can you take Mr Rutherford to make a statement?" he asked. "Is that okay with you, Cornelius?"

"I'll go anywhere as long as I can sit down and have a cup of tea," replied the solicitor as Tom led him down the corridor to the interview rooms. "And when this is all over, you owe me a very large Scotch, Shadow."

"What was all that about?" asked Jimmy. Shadow handed him Cornelius's piece of paper.

"It seems Rohan tried to reimburse those who lost money because of Spencer and Francesca."

"What about this last amount?"

"I think that's the account Rohan used for himself, although it's rather more than he suggested in the letter. I don't know about the Marquess of Granby; it seems like he's been playing at being Robin Hood. Phone the two Janes and ask them to look into it, will you?"

No sooner had Jimmy dialled the number than Stanley walked up the stairs from the custody suite. Before Shadow could say anything to him there was an excited squeal and Lottie rushed across the reception area and threw her arms around her father's neck.

"Where did she come from?" whispered Shadow, but Jimmy was too occupied speaking on the phone and happily watching the reunion.

"Dad! I'm so pleased they let you go and guess what?" gushed Lottie. "An agent has been in touch. He's a friend of the Dawsons. They were so impressed with my performance that they sent him a copy of the recording. Only the first half, obvs, but this agent really liked it and said he wants to represent me."

Shadow smiled and shook his head at her excitement and the selfishness of youth, but Stanley didn't seem to mind that his own ordeal had been forgotten. He planted a kiss on her head and said, "That's wonderful, love. Let's get home and you can tell me all about it."

Shadow was about to try to explain that Stan would get home to find his bank balance had increased substantially when Len Horning hurried through the door. His face was nearly as flushed as Cornelius's had been and was clashing horribly with the yellow jacket that he'd teamed up with bottle-green cords and polo neck.

"Thank heavens you are here, Chief Inspector. The strangest thing has happened. You will never believe me when I tell you."

"Your bank account has been credited with two hundred and fifty thousand pounds from Spencer Knight's account."

"Yes! But I swear his death had nothing to do with me."

"We know that, Mr Horning. We have a full confession from Rohan Kapoor."

"Rohan killed Francesca and Spencer?" asked Lottie, her eyes wide in surprise. "I don't believe it!"

"Are you sure, Chief Inspector?" asked Stan, looking equally stunned. "He's such a nice lad. Can we speak to him? Check he's all right in the head?"

"As I said, we have a full written confession from him, but I'm afraid you can't speak to him, as he isn't here. We believe he may have left the country at around the same time the money was being transferred into your accounts."

"Oh, I am pleased," said Lottie then flushed. "I mean I know it isn't good for you, Chief Inspector, but I would hate to think of poor Rohan languishing in a cell."

She seemed unconcerned that her friend had admitted killing the man whose death she had been so upset about.

"When did you last see him?" asked Shadow.

"It was after we left here. We went over to Harkers. Rohan bought me a drink and a sandwich then dropped me off at home. I found the note Dad had left and I felt awful. I called Rohan but there was no answer. I thought it was weird he didn't call back, but it makes sense now."

"Chief Inspector, you said accounts, plural," interrupted

Len.

"Yes. I understand that two hundred and fifty thousand pounds has also been credited to Mr Beresford's account."

"Blimey!" exclaimed Stan.

"So I can keep it? All that lovely dosh?" pressed Len, suddenly looking a lot more cheerful.

Shadow held up his hand. "As I'm sure you'll appreciate, this is a very unusual situation. The executor of Spencer's estate will be consulting with the bank regarding the best course of action, so I would caution you not to make any extravagant purchases until we have completed…"

He didn't bother to finish his sentence. Len, Stan and Lottie were already out the door, hugging and kissing each other with Len loudly declaring the drinks were on him.

"Well, they seemed happy and at least something positive might have come out of all this," said Jimmy cheerfully after ending his call. "And good news for Lottie. It sounds like she'll make it without Spencer's help. It goes to show true talent shines through. Everyone said she was easily the best actor in the pantomime."

"She was, although when it comes to playing a part convincingly, I think Rohan could give her a run for her money. He had the harmless, hapless, helpful young man down to a T."

"How did you work out it was him?"

"I read Kitty's statement."

Jimmy's face fell. "Did I miss something?"

"No, you weren't there when Rohan told me his laptop had been stolen. It was my fault. I should have paid more attention to the children's statements and read Kitty's sooner."

His sergeant reached over and patted him on the shoulder.

"Don't be too hard on yourself, Chief. He fooled us all. Tom's shocked and we both feel bad that we vouched for him. You might have been more suspicious of him if we hadn't. Angela and Mum won't believe it either."

Shadow nodded, but if anything, his sergeant's sympathy made him feel worse. It wasn't often he felt defeated by a case, but Rohan had been one step ahead of them all the time. Why? Was he distracted by Maggie being away or worrying about the rising river or was his heart simply not in this case because he found the victims so unsympathetic? He should have looked into Rohan's background and not simply accepted everyone telling him what a nice guy he was and how he had no possible motive to murder the victims. Had he subconsciously shared the killer's belief that the world was a better place without Spencer and Francesca in it? He gave his head a sharp shake. That was no way to start thinking. Only a few days ago he'd told Jimmy they weren't there to make moral judgements. He wasn't going to give up. There was still a chance they could catch him. He turned to Jimmy, who was fiddling with his phone and no doubt filling in Sophie on the morning's events.

"You had better get on to Interpol. Give them all the information we have and tell them to focus their search on India or Brazil."

"Brazil?"

"Rohan told me he was going to work in some sort of animal sanctuary there. There's a chance it might be true, I suppose."

"How would we organise extraditing an Indian national from Brazil?"

"With great difficulty, and I'm sure Rohan knows that too."

He left Jimmy to contact Interpol while he collected Cornelius's statement from Tom, then trudged back up to his office. He would have to inform the chief constable that they had a full confession but had managed to lose the killer. Mercifully, apart from the press office nagging, headquarters had been remarkably quiet, and it was with some relief that he heard the chief constable's secretary tell him that she was unavailable.

He set about writing his report while he waited for her to return his call. About an hour later, Jimmy arrived with an update.

"There's a record of a R Kapoor taking a KLM flight from Manchester to Rio yesterday evening. No definite confirmation that it was him though, and it's already landed, so…"

"The chances of catching him are close to zero," finished

Shadow. It was as he'd feared. "Anything else?"

"Yes, Chief. The Janes looked into the Marquess of Granby account, and you were right. It was emptied and closed this morning. They haven't been able to find the number or the locations of the accounts – just the references Rohan used. About a hundred grand was transferred to an account with the reference R Kapoor, but the rest, over half a million, was sent to an account with the reference *Nueva Vida Manta*. I remembered what you said about an animal sanctuary in Brazil and thought it might have something to do with manta rays, but then Jane said it wasn't Portuguese but Spanish."

"Which Jane?" asked Shadow.

"The slightly shorter one. Jane Silva, her dad's Portuguese. He moved back there and opened a hotel when he and Jane's mum got divorced but she goes out there all the time."

Shadow held up his hand before he learnt any more about half of the finance team's family arrangements.

"Did she happen to tell you what those Spanish words mean?"

"Yes, chief. '*Nueva Vida Manta*' means 'new life blanket', but that doesn't make much sense. I still think it has something to do with rescuing or rehabilitating animals."

Shadow sighed. Unlike Jimmy, he was struggling to imagine Rohan transferring his skills from tending to a pampered whippet to rehabilitating large tropical fish.

"So now we have to trace a bank account, possibly for a

sea-life sanctuary or possibly some sort of cloth manufacturer, somewhere in the Spanish-speaking world?"

"I know it doesn't sound great when you put it like that, Chief, but I'm sure the Janes will come up with more details and I'm going to keep looking into manta rays. There can't be that many rescue centres for them."

"I agree, but even if we find where the money went, it doesn't follow that we will find him. The story about going to work in South America could simply have been another red herring."

"No, I think it's like you've said earlier. The best lies always have a nugget of truth. If we find that half million, I bet we find Rohan."

As Jimmy practically jogged out of the office to continue his mission, Shadow wished he could share his confidence. His growling stomach told him it was lunchtime. In the past, he had been reliably informed that the chief constable spent her lunch hour jogging around Northallerton. It was probably safe for him to nip out and get something to eat.

The pale wintry sun was trying its best to break through the wispy clouds as he headed towards the Shambles pie shop. Making his way back with a pork pie in one pocket and a steak and ale in the other, he paused as he passed Bettys shop window. Their display was always eye-catching but today his attention had been caught by several boxes of shortbread biscuits, cut and decorated to look like various animals. There were cats, dogs, butterflies and ponies. They reminded him that there was someone he needed to thank. He stepped inside, purchased two boxes of the pony biscuits and glanced wistfully through to the restaurant before leaving and quickly heading down Stonegate.

He arrived at the Minster School to find the children careering around the playground making the most of the dry weather on their lunch break. Muffled up in a thick coat and hat with her hands wrapped around a large mug of tea, Angela was supervising them. She raised her hand in acknowledgement and came over to the gates when she saw him.

"Hello, Chief Inspector. What brings you here?"

"I brought the dwarves, I mean the children, some biscuits to thank them for their help. It turned out to be invaluable."

"That's very kind of you. They'll be thrilled. Thank you very much. Would you mind leaving them at reception? I can't leave my post." She lowered her voice. "I still don't know what I'm going to tell them about Rohan. I couldn't believe it when Tom told me. I thought he was so lovely."

"You weren't the only one," Shadow muttered as he waved her goodbye and headed towards the main entrance. He introduced himself to the receptionist and explained why he was there. Unlike the other receptionists he'd encountered recently, she was polite and efficient as she relieved him of the biscuits. On his way back down the corridor, he noticed the children's work displayed on the walls. To the right were various drawings of animals labelled with the French names and to the left was a map of the world with little flags pinned to their corresponding country. He paused to peer at the map, focusing on South America, wondering if there was anything in Jimmy's conviction that was where Rohan had gone. Where could manta rays be found anyway? Then he saw it. In Ecuador. Manta. A city on the coast.

He found his sergeant hunched over his computer scrolling through images of tropical fish on the screen.

"Manta is a city in Ecuador," said Shadow by way of a greeting.

Jimmy looked up. "Really? Fantastic. That must be where he's gone."

"It might be nothing to do with Rohan but look into it. At least find out if there is an airport there and let the Janes know too."

"Will do, Chief, and while you are here, we got some information back from the local taxi firms. I asked if any of them had picked up a man answering Rohan's description last night. There was only one under the name of Herriot."

"Rohan is a fan of the writer," replied Shadow immediately.

Jimmy's face lit up. "Really?" He began reading from the notes. "It was only to the station, but the driver remembered the man had a large suitcase with him and was in a rush to catch the train to Manchester Airport. He said his flight was leaving at eleven, but not where he was going to."

"See what flights left around that time."

Jimmy started tapping away at his keyboard. "There was one to Toronto and another to Quito. Where's that?"

"It's the capital of Ecuador," replied Shadow and immediately dodged out of the way as Jimmy punched the air.

"Yes! It's got to be him."

"No, it doesn't. When it comes to Mr Rohan Kapoor, I've learnt not to be certain about anything until I have some solid proof. Get on to the airline and find out what you can."

He returned to his office, not allowing himself to share Jimmy's excitement. Rohan had been several steps ahead of them from day one and even if they had found which country he was in, it didn't mean they were going to catch him.

He remained in his office for the rest of the afternoon and it was almost dark by the time he'd finished the report. There had been no further news from Jimmy and still no call from Northallerton. He was considering whether he should try phoning again when there was a cheerful knock on his door and Sophie appeared.

"Hi, Chief. Jimmy's convinced he's on to something with this place in Ecuador." She lowered her voice. "And I think he's feeling guilty about vouching for Rohan. He's waiting for a call from the British consulate out there, so I'm going send out for a takeaway. Can I order you anything?"

"No thanks, Sophie. I'm still waiting for the chief constable to call me back."

"You'll be waiting a long time. She's over in Portugal staying with Donaldson at his villa," said Sophie.

Shadow suddenly felt like a weight had been lifted off his shoulders. "Sophie, if you weren't a married woman, I might kiss you." He slapped the folder in front of him closed and stood up. "You'd think her secretary could have told me she was away. I've been sat here all afternoon."

Sophie smiled sweetly. "She was probably getting her revenge for all the times you haven't returned their calls."

Shadow allowed himself a wry smile too. She had a point.

"Maybe, but it does mean I can go and get something to eat, then go home and get changed," he replied. Sophie had the good grace not to mention his night spent in the station and simply nodded. "Ask Jimmy to call me if he does happen to strike gold in Ecuador, will you?"

"Of course. Have a good evening," she replied, closing the door behind her. Shadow pulled on his jacket, then groaned as he remembered *Florence* was still at Naburn. He seemed to face nothing but obstacles today. He peered out of the window into the semi-darkness. At least the river levels had fallen during the day and it would be safe to move her.

As he passed through reception, Tom called out to him. "Chief! Jake dropped some keys off for you and he said he'd left her where he found her. Does that make sense?"

"It does, thank you," Shadow replied, picking up the keys to *Florence*. "That's the second bit of good luck I've had today. It's about time."

"You know what they say, Chief. Good luck comes in threes. At least my gran says that."

"Then let's hope your gran's right and someone finds Rohan for us," replied Shadow, waving Tom goodbye and feeling more cheerful than he had all day. Before returning to *Florence*, he remembered he needed to collect his shirts from the laundry. He glanced at his watch. If he hurried, he should just make it before they closed. He was grateful that the rain and snow that had plagued the city all week had finally stopped as he walked briskly past the Minster and down Goodramgate.

As he passed the window of the Royal Oak a flash of bright yellow caught his eye. He paused and peered inside. Len Horning was standing at the bar, regaling his audience with some tale or other. To his left, grinning broadly, was Danny from the golf club and sitting in front of him were Stanley and Lottie with Arthur curled up on her knee. But they weren't the only ones there. Susan Edmundson was perched on a bar stool sipping a glass of champagne and sharing a joke with the major.

He considered going in and reminding them that there was a very good chance they would have to give the money back, then he watched as Stan turned and smiled at his daughter. It was an easy, unguarded smile. A smile Lottie probably hadn't seen for a long time. He didn't have the heart to spoil their moment of happiness. His stomach growled loudly as if agreeing it was time to move on and he turned and crossed the road. The phone in his pocket beep ominously. He fished it out and peered at the screen. It was a text from Jimmy.

> I think we've got him, Chief! Passenger flying from Rio to Manta on Indian passport under name of Manners. Do you get it? Manners was the name of the Marquess of Granby. Remember you told me about him? Flight lands midnight our time. Local police on standby! Will keep you posted.

Even his sergeant's text messages were overly long, but now it was Shadow who couldn't help smiling. Perhaps Rohan wasn't quite as clever as he thought. His fondness for aliases had finally tripped him up. He considered returning to the station then remembered Sophie's comment about Jimmy wanting to make amends. Shadow didn't think his sergeant had anything to make amends for, but if being in charge of liaising with the authorities in Ecuador made him feel better, he wouldn't interfere. For once Jimmy's optimism might be about to pay off.

With his mood improving by the minute, he pushed open the door of the laundry, then stopped. Maggie was standing behind the desk. All of a sudden, the party in the pub and even Jimmy's text didn't seem so very important.

"You're back!" he said.

"I can see why they made you a chief inspector," she replied, not bothering to look up from the laptop she was tapping away on.

"I didn't know you were home. I mean I've just come to pick up my shirts."

Maggie lifted up his bag of clean laundry and placed it on the counter.

"Will you be taking them back to the station? A little bird tells me you've been staying there."

"I fell asleep there last night, that's all," he replied defensively. "I'd been working late on the Knight and French case, and *Florence* was at the marina and that particular little bird is going to find himself on his way to Ecuador if he isn't very careful."

Maggie paused and peered at him over her reading glasses. "Why Ecuador?"

"We think that's where our murderer has gone. It was the young lad who was working for Owen Treadwell, Rohan Kapoor. He was avenging his uncle, apparently. He disappeared before we could arrest him but there's a good chance he's in Ecuador."

"You wouldn't really send Jimmy out there, would you? He and Sophie have only been married a few weeks," protested Maggie.

"I don't see why not. He's always griping about being cold here and besides it would serve him right. He had a bet on me not coming back from Italy."

"He wasn't the only one."

"Why would you think I wouldn't come back? I'd gone

out there to say goodbye, like you told me." His voice sounded gruffer than he had meant it to. "If you have finished here, shall we go and get something to eat?"

Maggie closed her laptop down and shrugged. "Why not. My fridge is so empty it looks like you own it."

He waited patiently as she bustled about turning appliances off and checking this and that before switching on the alarm and shooing him outside as the beeps counted down.

"Rohan seemed like such a nice boy. I met him when I went to the vet's with my sister to get her new kitten inoculated. Incidentally, the kitten is the reason I'm home early. She tripped over it and broke her ankle, the clumsy thing. Anyway, she's having an operation tomorrow and she'd need someone to look after her."

Shadow thought it was odd Maggie's sister couldn't have asked one of her children to look after her instead but decided it was best to remain silent and try to look sympathetic. He didn't want Maggie to think he wasn't pleased she was home.

"Don't you ever wish you could let them go?" she asked as they stepped outside and she turned the key in the lock.

"The killers?"

Maggie wrinkled her nose. "That sounds too harsh. What do the Americans say? Perpetrator – that sounds nicer."

He considered her question and let his mind sift through various cases he'd been involved with before nodding.

"Occasionally I have felt sorry for the perpetrator. Sometimes if they were acting to protect someone they loved or indeed if they didn't have long to live themselves."

"But not in this case?"

"No. I agree, Rohan did seem like a nice enough lad and what happened to his uncle was very sad. But he isn't the only person for whom things didn't turn out the way they would have liked. If we all went around killing those we blamed for our lives being less than perfect, where would we be?"

Maggie sighed.

"I don't think I would make a very good police officer."

Shadow smiled and shook his head. "No, but I've often thought you would make an excellent social worker."

"Really?" She seemed pleased at this idea. "If only I hadn't quit school at sixteen."

"If only. How many sentences of regret start with those two words?"

They paused for a moment as a large group of whooping and cheering students still in their gowns and mortar boards from their graduation passed by. Maggie took his arm as they walked on.

"Right, that's enough of being maudlin," she said firmly. "Where are you taking me? Catania's or Francesco and Lucia's place?"

"Actually, I thought we might try a new tapas bar on Fossgate Sophie was telling me about," he suggested and enjoyed seeing the look of surprise on her face.

"Tapas bar?"

"Well, you seem to be very struck with everything Spanish. Rather than have you disappearing off again, I thought I'd try to bring a bit of the Costa Blanca lifestyle to North Yorkshire. We can start with the food, but the weather might take a bit more work."

"You're seriously choosing Spanish food over Italian?"

"Paella can't be that different to a risotto and I've been sampling Rioja while you were away. It isn't too terrible. What do you think?"

"I think I'm lost for words."

"Well, that must be a first, so in this instance, I'm taking silence as agreement."

Then with a slight smile he led her towards the restaurant with the red and yellow flag fluttering in the dark.

The End

Want more? See the next book in the Bourbon Falls series, *A Stolen Shadow*!

Join Tule Publishing's newsletter for more great reads and weekly deals!

Acknowledgements

Thanks so much to everyone at the incredible Tule Publishing:

Jane Porter, Meghan Farrell, Cyndi Parent and Mia Gleason.

I am very lucky to work with an amazing team of editors who offer endless advice and encouragement.

Thank you, Sinclair Sawhney, for the great idea about adding the author's note. Thank you, Helena Newton and Beth Attwood, for your eagle eyes and your patience when it comes to my inexplicable use of commas!

Many thanks also to Lee Hyat and Patrick Knowles for coordinating and designing another perfect book cover.

I also want to thank everyone who has read and reviewed my books over the years, particularly Sam, Chris and Rekha, who have been with me from the start. I am so grateful for your incredible support.

A Stolen Shadow Crossword

Across

2. *Emma flies into Peru capital for this festive farce (9 letters)*
5. *The foot had the middle stolen (5 letters)*
7. *Pete initially used this portable device to contact a pal (6 letters)*
8. *A vole to adore (4 letters)*
9. *Eve can partly generate revenge (9 letters)*

Down

1. *Cash is my one vice (5 letters)*
2. *No sip, Olive! It could kill you (6 letters)*
3. *One MD uses heat to make an opioid (9 letters)*
4. *Her fat pater (6 letters)*
6. *Bears' claws may be as sharp as this sword (5 letters)*

A Stolen Shadow Crossword Solution

				1. M							
2. P	A	N	T	O	M	I	3. M	E			
O				N			E			4. F	
I				E			T			A	
S			Y		5. T	H	E	F	T		
O						A				H	
N						D			E		
	6. S		7. L	A	P	T	O	P		R	
	A						N				
	B			8. L	O	V	E				
	R										
9. V	E	N	G	E	A	N	C	E			

If you enjoyed *A Stolen Shadow,*
you'll love the next book in….

THE CHIEF INSPECTOR SHADOW SERIES

Book 1: *A Long Shadow*

Book 2: *A Viking's Shadow*

Book 3: *A Ghostly Shadow*

Book 4: *A Roman Shadow*

Book 5: *A Forgotten Shadow*

Book 6: *A Christmas Shadow*

Book 7: *A Stolen Shadow*

Available now at your favorite online retailer!

More books by H L Marsay

The Lady in Blue Mysteries series

Book 1: *The Body in Seven Dials*

Book 2: *A Death in Chelsea*
Coming in February 2024

The Secrets of Hartwell series

Book 1: *Four Hidden Treasures*

Book 2: *Four Secrets Kept*

Book 3: *Four Silences Broken*

Available now at your favorite online retailer!

About the Author

H L Marsay always loved detective stories and promised herself that one day, she would write one too. She is lucky enough to live in York, a city full of history and mystery. When not writing, the five men in her life keep her busy – two sons, two dogs and one husband.

Thank you for reading

A Stolen Shadow

If you enjoyed this book, you can find more from all our great authors at TulePublishing.com, or from your favorite online retailer.

Printed in Great Britain
by Amazon